DANGEROUS BOSS

WILLOW FOX

ONE

SADIE

Bang! A gunshot reverberates through the forest. It's in the distance. The trees canopy overhead as the sunlight is blocked by the thicket of leaves.

I should run in the opposite direction and stay as far from the dangerous situation up ahead, but there's only one trail, and turning around means I'll be hiking another ten miles.

I'm nearly back to my car.

Two miles to go.

My sister always told me not to go hiking alone. She warned me that dangerous men in the woods liked to snatch women and were involved in human trafficking rings.

Never hike alone.

She was always a bit overprotective. I don't blame her for her fears. She had a bad experience at college, dropped out, and moved home with Mom and Dad.

But we're nothing alike.

A second shot rings out, not quite in succession. Like there might have been a struggle. I can conjure up a dozen different scenarios in my head.

The tires squeal as dust kicks up, and the vehicle rushes away in haste.

I jog off the beaten path toward where the gunshots had erupted moments earlier. The vehicle is gone. The danger must no longer be imminent, either.

I don't know the exact spot. The trees all look the same. I'm unsure what I'm searching for when I stumble on his warm, lifeless body, tripping over him.

His complexion is pale as blood drips from his forehead. There's a fresh gunshot wound to his temple. Whoever shot him left him for dead.

I drop down onto my knees, searching for a pulse. It's faint, and sweat beads on his porcelain skin, mixed with blood.

Grabbing my cell phone from my pocket, I dial 9-1-1 and give my location as best I can, along with what I know, which isn't much.

"Hurry," I say.

The 9-1-1 operator doesn't have me hang up. She keeps me on the line. "Is he breathing?"

I lean down and can feel a soft breath expel from his lungs. "Barely," I say. "His pulse is really slow."

"Help is on the way. They should be there soon."

I put the phone on speaker and search through the dying man's pockets, looking for identification. There's no wallet on him. No keys. No phone.

Had someone driven him out here to kill him and dump his body?

Tattoos cover his arms. His beard is thick and matches his hair. There's a roughness, even while unconscious, that he echoes.

"Who are you?" I whisper.

He doesn't answer.

The EMTs arrive, and by the time they find us in the forest, off the beaten path, I'm not sure that the handsome stranger is still alive. I struggle to find a pulse. It's faint, but it's there.

I should walk away, return to my car, and never think about him again.

That would be a smart decision.

Someone wants him dead. If he survives, then that puts a wrench in their plans.

———

I get the hospital's name from the EMTs and hurry back to my car. Do I follow or head home and change?

Allie is spending the month at summer camp as a junior counselor with her friends, which at least gives me time to unravel the disaster that just happened.

I follow the ambulance to the hospital, not that I'm allowed in via the ambulance bay or double doors. I give what information I have to the hospital and am told to wait in the waiting room. I should go home and shower. Blood is caked to my jeans and stains my shirt.

At least it's not my blood.

Two police officers speak with the desk clerk before pointing at me. I press my lips together and inhale sharply on their approach.

"Ma'am, you were at the scene of the shooting?" the officer asks.

I stand, wanting to be at their level or closer as I answer their questions. "I heard gunshots," I say. I'm not comfortable divulging anything further. I don't know what happened and I'm not about to get mixed up in some war among thieves and dangerous men.

He is dangerous. I can sense it and should have bailed for my house the first opportunity I had after calling 9-1-1.

I'm not a monster. I wouldn't leave a man to die like the man in the vehicle. I can only assume it had been a man, unless it was a lover's quarrel that ended in attempted murder.

"Did you see anything?" the officer asks, taking out his notepad and pen to document my account.

"No."

"Do you know the gentleman's name who was shot?"

I shake my head. "No. I've never seen him before today."

"How many gunshots did you hear?" the officer asks.

"Two," I say, and the two officers exchange a silent glance. Only one has been speaking the entire time. The other appears younger, like he might be a rookie in training.

"And you didn't see any other victims or the perpetrator?"

"What? No." Had someone else been shot? Could it have been the driver who left the gentleman to die?

"What about a vehicle?" the officer asks. He taps the top of his pen on his notepad.

"A black SUV. It was dark and far away. It could have been navy," I recount, not remembering all that well. Tires squealed, and it had taken off hastily.

He jots that down and hands me his card. "If you think of anything else."

The two officers return to the front desk, say something to the woman, and then the double doors open and they are allowed into the back.

Are they intending to interrogate the stranger in the forest? I doubt he's capable of saying much, given his condition.

I sit back down in the scratchy, upholstered hospital waiting room chairs. There's a television on; the audio is muted, but closed caption is running. I can barely string two words together on the screen. My mind is in a haze.

An hour later, or maybe two hours, time seems to drift together, a doctor comes out behind the double doors. "Are you here with John Doe brought in earlier?" he asks, glancing at me.

The blood on my clothes is quite an indicator. "Yeah," I say.

The doctor approaches, and I inhale sharply.

Is it bad news?

Is he going to tell me that he didn't make it?

"We managed to remove the bullet, but given the swelling in his brain and fever, we've induced a coma. We'll continue to monitor his vitals and brain activity. He's not out of the woods just yet." The doctor grimaces at his remark. "Might I suggest you go home and shower if you plan on sticking around? We won't know anything for quite some time."

"Thank you," I say.

I heed his advice. Once he disappears through the double doors, I head out of the hospital and down to my car in the parking garage.

Why did I come here? What was I hoping to do?

I can't change what happened.

Anxious energy ebbs and flows through me. I can't sit still, and my hike did nothing to tire my ass out. It has to be all the extra adrenaline.

I drive home, across town, strip out of my clothes, and shower. Blood circles the drain. I'm relieved it isn't mine, but I keep seeing his face, blood pooling around his head.

The sound of tires squealing echoes in my mind.

Someone wanted him dead. But who? And why? I should stay far away from the hospital, from *him*, but I can't help my curiosity.

It doesn't help that my daughter, Allie, is away for the next several weeks. At her request, I sent her off to summer camp as a junior counselor. All her friends would be junior counselors this year, and she wanted to hop on the volunteer train and follow them.

Which I honestly don't mind. It's good for her to be out of the apartment for the summer. At thirteen, she's too young for a job, aside from the occasional babysitting gig she gets from the woman with a toddler down the hall in our building.

I douse myself under the spray, letting the stench and evidence of what I'd been mixed up in disappear with any lingering fear. I love crime dramas. I love movies filled with suspense. This is the ultimate mystery; I can't just sit and watch from the sidelines.

I want answers. And I'm not going to get them in my house.

After showering and dressing, I eat a quick bite before returning to the hospital. I have the afternoon off, and while I have a few errands to run and a house to tidy up, none of that seems important in the grand scheme of things.

A man nearly died today.

There were two gunshots.

Had there been a struggle after the first gunshot? Could that be the reason for the delay between shots fired? Or had someone else been shot as well? The police knew something, but they weren't talking.

What the hell happened out there in the forest?

————

I shower, dress, and return to the hospital. I wander to his hospital room and stand out in the hallway, peering inside.

There are no flowers. No guests or visitors at his bedside. The window shades are open, cascading a warm amber glow across the room. The harsh fluorescent overhead lights are off.

He's no longer donning his suit encrusted with blood on the collar. His eyes are closed. He lies motionless, asleep in a pale-green hospital gown, a white blanket covering him just past his waist.

His arms are at his side. Outside of the blanket, one arm is connected to an IV. Both are covered in tattoos, dozens of them with intricate artwork.

There are colorful wires tucked under his hospital gown, peeking out through his sleeves and the top of his gown hooked up to a monitor.

They're monitoring his heart rate and vitals.

He's silent, unmoving. Asleep.

The hospital bracelet on his left wrist denotes that he's *John Doe.*

My phone buzzes, and I grab my cell phone from my purse. A smile grazes my features that Allie is texting me. Shouldn't she be busy with crafts or water activities for the kids at camp?

Mom, is everything okay? Why are you at the hospital?

I tug my bottom lip between my teeth. I have a tracking app on my phone that lets me see where my daughter is. We have it set so that it goes both ways, and she can see my whereabouts too.

Yeah, just visiting a friend. How is camp? I text back.

What friend?

She avoids answering my question.

I'll tell you about it when you're home. There's too much to type, and I don't want to worry her. Besides, what exactly would I text, that I stumbled onto a handsome man being murdered and left for dead?

Sighing, I don't want to admit, even to myself, that he's handsome. Because that's not somewhere I'm willing to go.

I've avoided anything serious with a man since Allie was born. The thought of introducing her to a man makes my stomach flop, and I don't want her to get attached and heartbroken if it doesn't work out.

Allie is and has always been my priority. Above all else, I want her to be happy. And while she's older now and not around nearly as much, especially this summer, throwing myself into a summer fling seems like a bad idea.

A nurse steps into the hospital room, taking his vitals. "Are you family?" she asks, glancing me over. Her eyes are filled with hope.

I stall. If I say no, they likely won't let me stay. And why should I even be here?

My silence is answer enough.

She sighs softly and taps at the keyboard, recording his vitals. "It's nice he has someone at least," the nurse says, offering a weak smile.

I avert my gaze, glancing down at the gentleman lying in bed, asleep. His arms are covered in ink and at the top, peeking out from behind his gown, is a star tattoo. It's distinct. Bold. Unforgettable.

I've seen that star before. The image burns through my memory. It has to be a coincidence.

"Please, Aunt Sadie," Olivia begs, pushing the virtual reality headset into my hands.

"I'd rather watch you play."

"That's boring." Allie rolls her eyes. "No one wants to watch someone else play a video game."

Allie isn't wrong, but I'm terrible at video games. It's been years since I sat down with a Nintendo in front of a television. This is foreign to me. I take the white headset and place it over my head. Olivia comes up from behind, tightening and adjusting the straps for a snug fit.

"Is that good?" she asks.

The headset no longer bobs up and down. It's secure. "Yes. What am I supposed to do?" I ask.

She pushes the controllers into my hands. "Click on the box for Orc Hunter."

Orc Hunter happens to be her favorite game. Shooting orcs, dragons, and other mythical creatures with a bow and arrow. Olivia has managed to convince Allie to play as often as possible with her when they're together.

"Mom, can we get a headset too? It'd be so much fun to play with Olivia when we're not together," Allie says.

I knew she wasn't just letting me play because sitting and watching is boring. The girls always have some scheme concocted. Even as kids, they tried to set me up with my next-door neighbor. He was the closest male in proximity *who was single. The only thing we had in common, we both liked dating men.*

I click the box for Orc Hunter and wait for the game to load. "Are you sure you don't want to play?" I ask, trying to pawn the headset back on Olivia or Allie.

Olivia chuckles but doesn't back down. "Nope, it's all you. We can cast onto my phone, so I can see what you're doing when you play."

"Wonderful," I mutter under my breath. The girls will be able to make fun of me.

"Click on Multi-Player," Olivia instructs as she watches from her phone.

"Seriously?" I haven't even learned how to play, and she's throwing me in with other people.

"You have to learn sometime." Allie giggles.

"Just pick a room that is open," Olivia says. She's been playing Orc Hunter for a while.

Four games are open, and I jump into one on wave 34. That is the lowest wave I see, which I assume means level.

I jump into the game, and it takes a couple of minutes to get the hang of shooting with the bow and arrow. The controller vibrates slightly with tension as I pull back the bow. I aim and shoot, completely missing my mark.

Orcs stalk toward the gate in various colors, from bright orange, like Cheetos, to gray, spiky helmet goblins.

"Hey, Olive," a young female voice chimes through the headset.

"Hello?" I didn't realize that there was a microphone on, and the other players can hear me!

"My aunt is playing," Olivia shouts from nearby. She's far enough away to ensure I don't knock into her since I can't see anything outside the headset but loud enough for the other player to overhear.

I shoot an orc in the chest. "Why didn't he die?" The orc lifts the ax in his hand and throws it at my head.

"Duck!" Olivia shouts.

But it's too late.

I grimace and wince as a screen of red warns me that I'm out.

"It's okay. You'll come back in the next wave," Olivia encourages as I stand there staring at the scoreboard.

I suck, but it could be worse for my first time playing.

And I don't want to admit that even playing for a few seconds was a lot of fun.

Another player jumps into my box where I'm standing and shoots me with an arrow. "You're back," he says. He has a thick Russian accent, and it's evident in his tone that he's not a child.

"What?" I'm momentarily stunned, unsure what to do.

"Shoot orcs," he commands. His username pops up in small orange letters when he speaks: Bearded Bad Boy.

Inwardly, I groan. Of course that's his screen name. Except boy doesn't quite describe the voice I hear. It should be man. Bearded Bad Man. No, that doesn't have quite the same ring to it.

"On it." I turn toward the gate where the orcs are approaching and string my bow, firing one shot after another. My aim isn't much better, but I at least duck to avoid the next ax thrown at my head.

"You're a quick study," Bearded Bad Boy says.

I have half a mind to ask him what makes him such a bad boy, but Olivia is in the room, and I don't need our brief conversation turning dirty.

Gosh, it's been too long since I've conversed with a man, let alone bedded one. My thoughts are far too impure. Maybe taking my mind off the sound of a sexy man's voice and focusing on shooting mythical creatures will help.

As we slaughter all the orcs, the wave ends, and twenty seconds later, the next wave begins when it pops up on the screen, wave 35. There isn't much time for a break.

"Shit," I curse, glancing up as several green dragons fly across the sky. The Russian and the younger girl who seems to know Olivia shoot them down. I breathe a sigh of relief as I shoot at the incoming orcs as they tread across the bridge.

Each level grows more complex and more intense. "You're not too bad for a newb," the Russian says.

"First time," I say with a laugh. At least they're not asking me to leave so another player can come in and play. I wouldn't feel bad if they did. I royally suck.

The game is fast-paced, but we don't make it much longer as a giant red dragon blows fire on the other players, leaving me to save the gate.

And I fail epically. "Good game," the Russian says. I toggle the button to quit and remove the headset, my blood boiling.

"Does your mom know you play this game with grown men?" I can't fathom that my sister has any idea what her daughter is up to online.

Olivia scoffs and grabs the headset and controllers from me in haste. "It's fine. It's not like we're trading nudes. Don't be like Grandma."

"Caring?"

"Controlling and overprotective," Olivia says. "I know not to give my address to a grown man on the internet. Relax, it's fine."

"It's not fine. You don't know who you're conversing with within that game!" How can she be so willy-nilly, like it's no big deal?

"Sure I do. I play all the time."

"Fine, then who's the Russian who was playing? He's a grown man."

"He's on all the time. Usually only for a wave, and then bails. He must have liked you to keep playing until the town was destroyed."

I ignore Olivia's remark. She's trying to smooth things over because she's aware that her mother isn't going to take kindly to the news.

"Give me the headset," I say, holding my hand for the device.

"Fine," she grumbles, and pushes it into my palms. I secure the device and power it on, using the controllers to navigate through the main menu. There has to be a setting to block a player. I find the input screen where I can view and invite other people.

His screen name isn't hard to remember. I type in 'Bearded Bad Boy,' and immediately, an image pops up. Where it should be a profile picture, instead, it's a tattoo of a star. It's detailed and intricate and impressive if he designed it himself.

Which I doubt he did.

I don't know much about tattoos, but I'd bet that's not the only one that Bearded Bad Boy has on him, and there's no way in hell I want my innocent niece discovering any other ink on his body.

His profile is considerably empty. There's no first name, no description—just the close-up of a tattoo and the option to add him as a friend.

Nope.

It is not going to happen.

"Well?" Olivia quips, waiting for me to say something.

"I ought to block him," I say.

"What? Why? He's never said or done anything inappropriate. You're overreacting, Aunt Sadie."

I opt not to block him. He didn't say or do anything while I was online. Not that I want to tell Olivia that she's right. I exit the profile screen and power down the game before removing the headset. "Thirteen-year-old girls and grown men don't mix. Men like Bearded Bad Boy don't show up on the console just to play games."

"Yes, they do. I'll prove it to you. Buy a second console, and you can play every night when I'm online. You'll see that no one is harassing me or violating me. It's a safe space."

I exhale a heavy breath. "How about no video games while you're at my house?"

"Mom, you're being so mean."

"But I'm visiting for a month," Olivia whines. "That's going to be torture! I have friends online whom I chat with, and we hang out." Her eyes widen, and the young girl's eyes water.

I've seen the difference between real tears and the waterworks to get her way. These are genuine tears, which makes it that much harder.

"I know it seems silly and stupid to you, Aunt Sadie, but gaming gives me something to do. And it's exercise. You can't tell me you're not sore from Orc Hunter."

My arm is a little sore, and I'll bet my legs will be aching tomorrow from all the squats I did to avoid getting an ax thrown at my head. "I'll watch you girls play and monitor your phones," I say.

"Okay, but when I'm asleep, you can borrow my headset," Olivia says with a grin, glancing at Allie.

"That's not necessary."

A smirk lights up Olivia's face. "A few hours of playing Orc Hunter this week, and you'll be addicted."

"Maybe we should find some other activities to do outdoors," I say.

"Mom," Allie whines. "I promise it's good for the soul."

"Playing video games?"

"Exercise, mental stimulation, meeting new people. You always say I should make new friends," Allie says. "This is what I'm doing, with Olivia's help."

I grumble under my breath. "No more chats with grown men."

———

I dig my fingers into the armrest of the hospital chair, staring at the tattoo peeking out from the hospital gown on his chest.

It's probably a coincidence that he has the same star tattoo. He'd mentioned it once when I asked him about the profile picture online.

"Are you stalking me?" he asks as I join him in the VR game Orc Hunter.

I laugh under my breath. "I don't even know where you live. So, no. I can't be stalking you."

"Right." He chuckles, and I swear he's smiling. But I can't see him, only his avatar in the game, and he's not that close. He's across from me, guarding the opposite tower on the other side of the town as we shoot at orcs. "Isn't it early where you are?"

"It is," I say. The sun has just risen, and my niece and daughter are asleep. She won't wake until at least ten o'clock, if not later. Which gives me a couple of hours to see what the fuss is all about regarding her virtual-reality gaming.

I don't tell the stranger where I live or what time zone I'm in. The less he knows, the better. The last thing I want is to give him any information on my niece.

"What about you?" I ask. "Are you in Russia?" There are three servers; the one I connected to was in the USA. But anyone could join any server.

"Tit for tat."

"I'm not showing you my—"

He snorts and clears his throat. "I wasn't asking. You tell me where you're from, and I'll tell you where I live."

His accent is thick, heavy, and undoubtedly, he's from Russia, even if he's moved out of the country and residing elsewhere.

"I asked first," I say. It's like we're in the third grade, and I roll my eyes, realizing how ridiculous this conversation sounds between two grown adults. My attention is on the dragons, shooting them first and then the orcs, ducking as they throw axes at my head.

Bearded Bad Boy is skillful at avoiding an ax attack. He jumps from one platform to another to avoid being slaughtered.

"Show off," I mutter.

"Jealous." There's amusement in his tone, like he's enjoying teasing me.

"No, I don't play this game all day."

"Neither do I," he says. "This is just a—hobby," he says, though he sounds unconvinced.

"Chatting with teenage girls is a hobby?"

"I don't know what game you're up to, but I can assure you that my interest is not the least bit in teenage girls, or boys, for that matter."

Relief should flood through me, but there's an anger in his tone. A forcefulness like I've offended him, and he's about to rock the boat. "And what about you? Do you enjoy making baseless accusations? You sound like a fed or a dirty cop."

"I'm not either of those things," I say. "Do you have something against authority figures?"

"Not so long as I'm the one in charge." He gives off an alpha vibe, like he's the one always calling the shots.

There's a silence that rains down over us; the only audio that echoes through the headset is the sound of killing orcs and the enemy, one shot after the next.

He's good. A little too good if you ask me, but I'm not a regular. Hell, this isn't even my headset. I'm playing on Olivia's game under her screen name. Not that she'll care, as long as the battery is charged when she wakes up.

Maybe I should impose some rules for the girls while Olivia is over. No gaming before noon.

The man in a coma could be Russian. But he could be any number of nationalities. The plethora of tattoos should help the hospital narrow down his identity.

The bandage on his forehead covers his scars as he lies entirely still, unmoving except for the rise and fall of his chest. I sit at his bedside, waiting for someone to show up, to recognize him and sit with him. Reaching out, I rest my hand on his arm.

His skin is cool to the touch. I pull the blanket up higher to help keep him warm. "Hang in there," I whisper. Whoever he is, he doesn't deserve to die or to be left for dead.

I glance at my phone. I could text my niece and ask her to let me know if *Bearded Bad Boy* comes online, not that it matters. What would I even tell the thirteen-year-old? I witnessed a man nearly dying, and I recognized he shares the same tattoo with an online player.

I'll sound insane.

Bearded Bad Boy never did tell me where he was from.

TWO

DMITRI

Six Weeks Later

My head really fucking hurts. I'm not talking about a slight headache that requires a couple of pills to dull.

The pain is immense, like someone took a jackhammer to my head and then decided to drill into my skull.

The smell of antiseptic permeates my senses first. I can't help but groan as my eyes lazily open to realize I'm in a hospital somewhere.

Her bright blue eyes widen as she stands from the seat at my bedside.

"You're awake," she says. Her eyes widen in surprise, and her complexion turns ghastly. She has a book in her hands, the binding worn.

"Do I know you?" Am I supposed to recognize the brunette? I swear if I've met her, I'd remember. It doesn't matter the headache and pain ripping through my skull. I'd never forget her face or body.

She gives a sheepish grin. "I found you in the forest. Shot."

I grimace and reach up to my head. There's no bandage. No pain, not like I'm expecting. "How long have I been here?" I get the distinct impression it's more than a couple of hours.

"About six weeks," she whispers, and glances away.

And she stayed with me the entire time?

Why?

"I've been reading to you," she says sheepishly, folding her other arm over the book to hide what she's been reading.

"What book?" I ask. I don't recall hearing her voice, let alone anything else about her, and I'd recognize her if we'd met any other time. She's young and delicate, and there's an innocence to her. I reach up to touch where I'd been shot, and my fingers graze the scar.

Her hands are delicate and soft as she brings my arm down, although my head doesn't hurt. "And you are?" I ask.

"Oh right, Sadie West," she says, and smiles. The girl has the most irresistible smile and dimples that give her the perfect girl-next-door vibe.

The things I could do to ruin little miss perfect.

"And you are?" she asks, waiting for me to answer.

I clear my throat and stall.

Someone wants me dead. I can't remember who shot me or what happened. I work for the Russian Bratva, and I had been ordered to murder Anton and his girlfriend, Savannah. Nikita had been with me in the car. But everything after that is behind a veil, kept away from my memory.

"You didn't have any identification on you," Sadie says.

"Can't remember." I try not to give an ounce of indication that I'm lying. "It's all a blur."

"I should let the doctor know that you're awake." She's cute, with a nice, pert ass I examine while she heads out of the hospital room.

It would be good if she left. I'm a dangerous man. She has no reason to stick around and spend time with me. I'm not good company.

The nurse comes in first, taking my vitals as the doctor enters a few minutes later.

Sadie stands in the hallway, watching, giving us space and privacy.

"Do you know your name?" the doctor asks.

"I don't," I lie. It's easier. The police will be investigating the shooting. The hospital is required to report any gunshot injuries, and we're not at Steele Concierge Medical, which means these doctors aren't bought or paid for by the bratva.

They are forced to report the crime to the police.

"How about what year is it?"

I relay the year and the doctor nods, pleased that I have that correct. She asks the same about the president, and I seem to get those questions correct. Maybe I should have played it off as more confused, but I don't want them running a million medical tests on me.

I want to go home.

Although where the hell is home?

I can't return to the compound with Mikhail running the shots. For all I know, he ordered my execution.

Did Nikita shoot Anton or me? Maybe Anton's girlfriend Savannah had a gun hidden on her, and she pulled the trigger? She did work for the feds.

Everyone is a suspect.

The doctor jots down a couple of notes and informs me that no lasting trauma is indicated on the tests they've already run, but they will have a neurologist examine me later this afternoon. She hurries out of the room to look in on another patient.

"Enjoying the hallway?" I quip, glancing at Sadie as she pretends to pick lint off her shirt.

"I didn't want to intrude," Sadie says, sneaking back into my room.

"Can I ask you something?" While I know my name, I don't recall what happened. She nods, letting me continue. "Was there anyone else?"

"What do you mean?" Sadie asks, staring at me blankly. The girl hasn't the slightest clue what I'm asking about. Of course, she wouldn't, because she doesn't know what went down in the forest.

Neither do I.

"When you found me. Was I alone?"

Sadie saunters farther into my hospital room. Her toes drag over the floor for a beat. There's something that she's hiding, but I don't know anything about her to figure out what that might be.

Did the Italians send her?

No. If they did, I'd be dead. She'd have suffocated me when I was asleep.

She slumps into the chair beside my bed. "Are you asking if I saw the shooter? Because I didn't." Her answer comes out a little too quickly and forced. Almost like she's rehearsed it in her head a dozen times.

Maybe she doesn't want to admit to witnessing what happened. She's smart if she plays that route and pretends not to have seen anything.

"I meant when you found me, was I alone?"

"Just you and the dirt," Sadie says. She quirks a wry grin before glancing down at her lap.

Why is she still here? If I ask her and I'm too brash, she might leave. And that's the last thing I want.

"Thanks for saving my life, bringing me here," I say, and gesture toward the room.

I hate hospitals. Not that I know anyone that likes them, but I despise them. Men die in places like this after bloodthirsty battles. I want to go home but can't return to the compound.

"You don't remember your name?" Sadie asks, shocked that someone could forget their identity. It'd be easier if I had complete amnesia, the kind you see in movies or read about, where the character forgets everything about themselves, including being the bad guy.

It's a shame that I can remember the countless horrific acts I've done in my life, but I can't recall what happened when I was shot.

"Can't say I do."

"You came in with no identification, no phone, not even a set of house or car keys." Sadie quietly sits beside me, her hands folded together in her lap. "What are you going to do when they release you from this place?"

"Hold up a convenience store and sleep in the back room?"

She doesn't smile or laugh.

"It's a joke," I say. Doesn't she get that? Not that she knows me. "Relax, I'll be fine. You don't need to stay and babysit me unless you're a cop?" Is that why she's still here, trying to pry information out of me?

Is she working on the investigation and wants to know who shot me? Well, I don't intend on pressing charges. That isn't how us bratva type work.

"I'm not a police officer. But an officer was looking to speak with you while you were in a coma. He left his card." She points at the business card on the nearby table. No flowers, get-well cards, or other gifts were sent to the hospital for me.

I chalk it up to the hospital, not having identified me, but what about the bratva? Did they leave me to die and not bother to recover the body? That's unusual and suspect. Something is amiss.

"What did you tell them?" I ask.

"That you were in a coma and needed rest."

"Good," I say, and sit up, pulling the IV line out of my arm. My head pounds from the sudden movement, but I can't sit around and wait for the cops to interrogate me. Will the hospital inform them that I'm awake?

"What are you doing?" Sadie's voice raises an octave.

I can't help but worry that she'll alert the authorities. "Getting the hell out of here."

The television is on. It's mostly been background noise, the news. I haven't paid much attention until I stand and sway in my less-than-stellar hospital gown. My feet are rubber, and my legs jelly. It takes all my effort to stand and not fall over. I'm weak, not that I'd ever admit it to anyone.

"Where are my clothes?" I can't leave the hospital with my ass hanging out in a gown.

"The doctors put your dirty clothes in a bag," Sadie says, and opens the wardrobe closet.

I stumble into the bathroom and slam the door. It takes no time to strip down. I'm practically naked already. I grimace as I rip the electrode stickers attached to my chest and pull on my black suit pants and white shirt. The collar is covered in crimson. There's a splatter of blood down the front of the shirt that dripped from the injury. My suit coat is wrinkled, but it'll cover most of the blood for the time being. I'll need new clothes, something less conspicuous.

Too bad Sadie didn't think to bring me a spare change of clothes.

When I emerge from the bathroom, Sadie's head is down, glancing at her phone. She tucks her cell phone into her purse and folds her arms across her chest. "I don't know what's going on, but you're not leaving. You can't."

I stop myself from telling her that she can't make me stay. My footing is wobbly, and perhaps Sadie senses my discomfort and imbalance. I grip the nearby wardrobe attached to the wall, letting it hold me up.

There's a heavy sigh that spills past her lips. She glances me over and tucks the book tight in one hand, and with her other hand, she escorts me toward the chair that she had been in earlier. "You'll stay with me," Sadie says.

"That's a terrible idea."

She scoffs under her breath. "When someone makes you a polite offer, there are nicer ways to decline. But with that said, I wasn't inviting you to stay in my home. I don't know you. But I work at the Luxenberg. I can get you a room."

"A hotel?" I slip on my shoes and socks. I'm not capable of standing and putting them on. The room sways as I sit, but I ignore the dizzying sensation.

When my shoes are on, I jump up and head out into the hallway. I sway from side to side like I'm on rough seas and trying to keep my balance. The nurses are busy, not paying the slightest bit of attention to a man walking out in a suit. Perhaps they'd have glanced up from their computer screens and charting if I had donned a hospital gown.

Sadie grabs my arm, accompanying me, steadying me from falling on my ass. With each step, my footing becomes more solid and less nauseating. I've always had an iron-clad stomach, but the room spinning around haphazardly doesn't help.

"You're improving," she says as we step into the elevator together.

"Fake it till you make it," I joke, and can't help but glance down at the book in her hand. She's covering the title, but it's a romance book with a half-naked man on the front cover. Was she reading me mommy porn? I think I like her already.

She presses the button for the lobby, and I lean back against the wall, letting it prop my ass up until we reach our destination. "What book did you bring?" I ask.

Her cheeks redden, and she brushes a stray lock of hair behind her ear. "Does it matter?" Her laugh is soft and light. She's embarrassed and avoids my question.

The elevator door opens, and she steps out first. I'm right behind her, and she links her arm to mine, escorting me through the long hallway and parking garage. It's quite a walk, but that's my fault, bolting out of there before any more tests are performed or questions asked.

I've never had to lie about who I am or my role. Yes, being part of the bratva has been a secret, but the company I usually keep is aware of my role.

This is new territory.

I was pretending to be a good guy.

I watch my surroundings every step through the hospital and to the garage. I have to be vigilant. There are enemies throughout the city who would love the advantage of taking me hostage, torturing me for answers regarding the bratva.

And Sadie is too innocent to get wrapped up in my drama. I don't want to see her get hurt.

"Get in," Sadie says as she unlocks the two-door hatchback. "Sorry, it's not super fancy," she says with a shy smile.

The yellow two-door hatchback has rust on the fender, and one of the taillights is busted. Was she in an accident, or had someone purposely smashed the light to harass her?

"It's perfect," I say, opting not to comment on her vehicle since she's kind enough to do me a favor and get me out of here. The longer I'm at the hospital, the more time there is to be discovered by Mikhail or his men.

The car is a rust bucket, and a small one at that. My knees are scrunched in the front seat, but at least it's a free ride. I can't exactly pay for a cab or a hotel. And I haven't even sat still long enough to consider that I have no access to my accounts without my identification or wallet.

This is going to be more complicated than I thought. I can pickpocket like the best of them, but that'll land me a few dollars, not enough to survive comfortably.

My stomach is heavy, and I wipe the sweat that coats my hands on my pants, every so often glancing in the side mirror for anyone tailing her vehicle.

Sadie blasts the air conditioning in the small car, but it's only hot, disgusting air that jets out from the vents. I push the vents in front of me away.

"It'll cool off in a few minutes," Sadie says.

It won't feel too soon, that's for sure. There are no parking fees in the garage, and Sadie drives haphazardly through the lot and out the exit.

Perhaps she's the reason for the busted taillight. Her driving leaves much to be desired. Next time, I'll offer to drive. Assuming there is a next time.

I shift uncomfortably in the front seat. The seatbelt is low and tight across my lap. It's suffocating, and the heat is stifling.

I'm familiar with the hospital we just left and the hotel where we're heading. It's at least a twenty-minute drive with no traffic, and the roads are rarely empty, except maybe when I would get off work at Club Sage.

My latest job for the bratva had been watching the door, a bouncer for the club. Although it was more flattering a position than just checking IDs and throwing scum-sucking men who got handsy with the dancers out. I was solely responsible for ensuring that members of the Italian Mafia didn't sneak inside. And in the early morning hours, when I finished at the club, I was responsible for making first contact with our buyers. The environment required secrecy, security, and no paper or electronic trail.

But things were finally on the up and up when I landed in the hospital with a bullet in my head.

Sadie tears through the city at lightning speed, blowing through a few lights just as they turn red. The girl is a natural-born terror.

It's highly arousing. She has me instantly hooked on her. Could it be that she saved my life, or is there something more lingering between us?

"Are you sure I can stay at the Luxenberg?" I ask.

There are worse places that I could stay. A hotel would at least be under the radar. The bratva aren't going to look for me at a hotel. Especially when they think I'm dead and all my credit cards and accounts are run through them—another reason to be grateful to have ditched my wallet.

Although that wasn't on purpose. At least I don't recall leaving it behind. I must have forgotten it on the job.

Her attention is on the road, her hands on the steering wheel as we jut through neighborhoods and down side streets, avoiding stopped traffic and lights, breezing right through two stop signs. "I work the front desk. I can check you into one of the rooms and just mark it as unavailable due to a maintenance issue."

Sadie has no idea what she's getting involved in by helping me. "I'll pay you back," I say. I don't like being in anyone's debt, even if it's a cute brunette. Owing someone a favor doesn't sit well with me.

"It's not a big deal. No one has to know," Sadie says with a smirk. There's a rebellious side of her that I find sexy as hell. All the members of the bratva are men. A handful of ladies live on the compound, girlfriends, and wives, but they're not members. In another life, she could have broken the mold and become one of the family.

Then again, Mikhail would never see to it that a member of the bratva would be a girl. He's the Pakhan, the leader of the Russian organization that operates in New York City.

"Do you need to stop and pick up some clothes?" Sadie asks.

It's not like I'm supposed to know where I live, and I don't have any house keys in my pocket. "That's a tough job, considering I don't remember anything," I say.

She clears her throat and glances briefly at me. "I can loan you a few dollars. We can stop by a Target or Walmart and see what fits you?"

I'm tall and robust, and while I'm sure there are jeans and t-shirts that I can purchase, I won't be wearing my usual suit and tie attire. Not that I particularly need to be in a suit coat lounging around the hotel. And where the hell else am I going to be able to go if the bratva is after me? I'll need to lie low and stay out of trouble.

Not something I excel at, given my expertise.

"I don't want to put you out," I say.

"You won't. You'll pay me back." Sadie gives me a thousand-watt smile. "If you need a job, you can always clean my apartment. I *hate* cleaning."

I groan under my breath. That's not the kind of work I enjoy doing. But I've done worse, cleaning up dead bodies—an apartment with dust and dirt, that should be a breeze. And maybe I'll even do a little snooping around. There's something about Sadie that I can't quite put my finger on. Probably the fact that she's here, willing to help me, and I've been in a coma for six weeks.

Who does that?

What kind of a person waits around for a stranger to wake up?

"You're too kind." And I mean every word of it. If she knew the kind of man I am, the things I've done, she wouldn't look at me with such a hopeful gaze. The girl is innocent, and just being around me will ruin her.

Sadie smiles, her hands on the steering wheel. Every so often, she glances at me like she's thinking something but doesn't want to say it aloud.

"What?" I have a knack for reading people, especially pretty young ladies.

"You don't remember anything?" Sadie quips. She pulls up to the Target parking lot and shuts off the engine. I'm relieved to climb out and stand, stretching my legs. I swear she bought a clown car. Sadie follows me to the front entrance, her arm linking with mine again. "I don't want you falling over, mister." She chuckles.

"I don't even remember my name." The lie is getting easier to tell as I'm trying to convince myself that I don't know who I am.

"That's wild." She glances me over as she stalks toward the carts. "Do you need to hold on, or are you okay?"

"I'm fine, but thank you for asking." I've gotten my land legs back, and while my head does throb, I ignore the sensation.

Convinced that I'm okay to walk on my own, Sadie grabs a cart and pushes it through the store, leading me toward the men's department.

Is the girl about to help pick out my wardrobe? It's a little too domestic for me, but I refrain from saying anything offensive. Sadie is trying to be helpful. I need her if I'm going to stay off anyone's radar.

I don't have to worry about the surveillance cameras recognizing me. I'm not a man who is wanted, and I'm pretty sure they all think I'm dead.

Anger sizzles inside of me, wanting answers. The report earlier on the news with Anton and Savannah has me itching to find access to the internet to do a little digging and reconnaissance of my own.

But I won't get those answers with Sadie at my side. She's too good, too kind and innocent to be around the violence and bloodshed amongst the bratva.

They used to be men whom I aligned myself with, but I no longer recognize myself or where I fit in the grand scheme of their organization.

I grab a few items off the rack, nothing that will stand out or be flashy. I don't need to put a target on myself. They think I'm dead. It's better to keep them unsuspecting.

I need a plan and a weapon.

I'm not likely to get caught without identification or contacting an old source who might give me up.

I'll get a knife later when I'm not having the cute little ray of sunshine tagging along—no sense in scaring the girl.

I clear my throat after dropping enough clothes for two days in the cart. "Let's go." I'm done shopping; this isn't my idea of fun, and the painkillers the hospital had me on are wearing off.

My mood is slipping with it, making me grumpy and anxious.

We're on the opposite side of town, nowhere near the compound, but I can't take a chance that I'll run into any members of the bratva.

My head swims just thinking about what it all means. Nikita was in the car with me in the woods. Did Anton and Savannah kidnap him? Kill him?

"Are you sure I was brought into the hospital alone?" It doesn't make sense. Why leave me to die and not Nikita, too?

"You're the only *hiker* I tripped over," Sadie says. However, she forces the use of the word hiker. She isn't an idiot.

Is she aware that I wasn't in the woods to go hiking?

"Why?" Sadie asks as she glances at me before brushing a strand of hair behind her ear.

She's nervous.

Why?

Do I scare her? Or does she know something that she's not saying?

"No reason." The less I say, the better. It's for her safety. There are men who want me dead, any number of men, least of all the bratva, which have somehow now been added to that list.

We finish shopping, she pays, and I feel guilty that I can't cover the essentials. I will pay her back, even if it means having to rob a bank to get her the funds. I drop the bags into the trunk of her tiny car. "I can drive," I offer.

"With that head injury?" She points at the scar on my head.

"It was weeks ago," I counter. I'd caught a quick glimpse of the scar in the reflection coming into the store through the glass doors. It doesn't look that bad.

"And your ass just woke up from a coma. No thanks. You can ride shotgun."

It's her car. And while I want to make her turn over the keys and demand she does as I say, the girl is helping me out. I should be thankful, which isn't an easy emotion to deal with, given my line of work.

"Yeah," I mutter, and climb into the front passenger side. I slam the door shut and yank the seatbelt tight across my waist, waiting for her to start the engine and pull out into traffic.

Every so often, she glances at me. I can tell she wants to ask me something because she keeps opening her mouth, and her tongue darts out, swipes across her lips, before she shuts her trap.

Smart.

Stay quiet.

It could save her life. Not that I intend to harm her. She's given me no reason to be a danger to her.

Besides, I'd never hurt a woman. There are some lines that I won't cross. Ditching her ass, however, is a very real possibility. But I need her help.

Sadie drives us haphazardly to the hotel. She parks the car a little too abruptly, forcing my seatbelt to lock. "Where'd you learn to drive?"

She laughs under her breath. "Come on, let's get you a room." She shuts off the car and climbs out.

I follow, waiting for her to unlock the trunk. Once she opens the lid, I grab my bags. I didn't buy much, and I will repay her every cent.

Sadie strolls into the hotel like she owns the place. Her confidence is unwavering. "Hi, Pauline." There's a friendliness to her that seems to fit her personality, like she's not just putting it on for show.

"I thought you were off today."

"I am, but I left my phone somewhere around here."

"Did you check the break room?" Pauline asks.

"I did not. Can you check it while I call my phone?" Sadie grabs the landline and begins to dial her cell phone.

"Of course," Pauline says, and wanders down the hallway.

While Pauline is busy trying to help track down Sadie's phone, she taps away at the computer. She grabs two hotel room keycards and programs the cards before tapping away again at the computer screen.

"Room 312." She hands me two room cards, and I shove one into my pocket and grip the second card.

"Thank you." My thumb brushes over her skin before I head to the elevator doors. It'd look suspicious if I hung around too long at the front desk without checking into a room.

I stalk toward the elevators, glancing back over my shoulder for Sadie. She offers me a warm smile, reassuring me that everything is fine. I hit the button for the elevator and wait for the door to open.

Pauline shakes her head, wandering back to the front desk. "Your phone isn't in the break room."

"I found it in the bottom drawer. I don't know how it got there." Sadie laughs. "Thanks for helping me look for it, Pauline." She steps around from behind the counter as the elevator door opens.

I step in and hit the button for the third floor. I can no longer see Sadie from my position inside the elevator. I want to steal one last glance at her, but I'm sure that if I'm staying at the hotel, it's not the last I've seen of her.

I lug my shopping bag with the few essentials up to my room. From the outside, the hotel is swanky yet old. But the inside has been recently remodeled and still smells of fresh paint. The carpet, even in the hallways, is still considerably plush.

I unlock the door to my room. There's a single king-sized mattress, which is more than perfect for my needs. I flip the lights on and abruptly shut the curtains, not wanting anyone to see inside. Even three stories up, I don't want to take any chances someone might be watching.

The small kitchen has a full-size refrigerator, a sink, and a stove. It's an efficiency, which is exactly what I need until I figure out my next steps.

Staying in New York is dangerous, but leaving and starting a new life, I have nothing. No job. No access to funds. I'm fucked. And I can't exactly put what I did for a living on a resume. There are no references to call. Hell, there's no leaving the bratva alive.

Except Mikhail and his men believe I'm dead.

I slump onto the edge of the mattress. My head falls into my hands.

I need answers.

Mikhail won't give them to me, but Nikita was the one in the car with me. Is he dead? Could he be working with Anton? Would Nikita betray Mikhail and the family?

Nikita is a good man, loyal to Mikhail, same as me.

None of it makes sense.

I can't pick up the phone. I don't want them to know where I'm hiding. It's bad enough that once I reach out to one of them, they'll know I'm still alive.

I leave the bag of clothes and toiletries on the bed and head toward the door. Already, the room is suffocating me. I need to do something. Sitting another minute isn't going to help.

Pulling back the door, I see that Sadie is standing on the opposite end.

"Hey, I didn't expect to see you again so soon," I say. What's she doing here?

"I brought you some towels." She has a stack of fluffy white towels in her hands and a bag of hotel toiletries. "Since you won't be getting housekeeping service, I thought I'd load you up with a few essentials. There's a toothbrush and toothpaste too."

"Are you trying to tell me something?"

She laughs nervously and pushes the items in my arms to take.

"Do you want to come in?" I ask as I grab the towels off her, turn to carry them into the room and drop them on the counter in the bathroom.

Sadie isn't the least bit nervous. She glances around the room, probably making sure everything is up to the standard that she would expect. "That isn't necessary." Shuffling her feet, I sense that something else is weighing her down.

"What is it? You didn't come up here to give me towels." There are probably a few towels already in the bathroom.

"I spoke with one of the officers at the hospital while you were in surgery," Sadie says.

I inhale a nervous breath and clear my throat. "And?" She wouldn't have assisted me if she knew anything about who I am or who I work for.

"And nothing. He was about as evasive as you are." She steps farther into my room, closing the door behind herself.

Her hands are empty. There's no weapon, but she doesn't seem to be backing down, either.

Did she intend on bringing me here to sell me to the cartel, the mafia, or the bratva? My instincts warn me that she could be dangerous, and bringing me here is entirely for her benefit.

I match her stare with silence. I refuse to answer her. As far as she knows, what I've said is the truth. I don't remember what happened. While I'd rather her think I still have some form of amnesia, I can't recall the shooting. Will I eventually? I have no idea.

"Hard to give many answers when I don't know who I am," I say. I give a nonchalant shrug and glance her over, stalking closer. I tower above her, invading her personal space as she's just inches from her back to the door. "If you don't mind, I have somewhere to be."

"And where is that?" Sadie asks. "You don't have any money, a job, or even know your name."

My jaw tightens at her question. "I'd like to take a walk, clear my head. Is that a problem?"

"Your head needs to be resting, along with the rest of you. Did you forget that you were shot?"

"Hard to forget," I mutter under my breath. "But that was weeks ago. I'm fine."

Her hands are on my chest, guiding me toward the bed. "Get in," she commands as she pulls back the covers.

"It's not even close to bedtime." She can't be serious. I'm not taking orders from *her*.

"You left the hospital against the doctor's orders. You ought to be resting until dinner."

"How do you know it was against orders?" I ask. It wasn't like I signed myself out of the hospital. I snuck out before anyone could notice.

She gives me a look that stares straight into my soul and makes me shift on my feet uncomfortably. "I'll take it easy, under one condition."

"And what's that?" she asks.

"You play nurse, and I'll stay in bed." I doubt she's interested. She's a good Samaritan, going above and beyond. Maybe she enjoys helping people for a living because she's a good person. I wouldn't know much about that. I'm no saint.

"I don't know what fantasy you have going on in your broken and bruised head, but I'm not wearing a nurse's outfit and coddling you like a child."

"Too bad," I say, and grin. She would look dynamite in a short white skirt that barely covered her ass.

"Wipe that smug smile off your face. I need to head out, but I'll be back later to check on you and bring dinner. But not because I'm your nurse. I'm not." Sadie retreats toward the door. Her bottom lip is tugged between her teeth. "Get some rest."

"Will do, boss," I joke with her. She's not the least bit intimidating.

THREE

SADIE

Before stopping for Chinese takeout, I head to my apartment to let my puppy out. Allie is back from summer camp but spending the day at her friend's house.

Stopping at my place, I grab the leash, secure it to Kona's purple collar, and head downstairs with her.

If the hotel weren't strict about their no-dogs policy, I'd bring her with me when I pick up dinner.

In under twenty minutes, Kona is walked and fed. I put in an order for takeout. I don't know what he eats, let alone his name. Am I supposed to call him *John*, as in *John Doe*? I order quite a few different dishes. He can save the leftovers and have the food for lunch and dinner the next couple of nights until things settle down.

I can't fathom what he's going through, not knowing who he is or where he belongs. My stomach is tangled in knots at the heaviness of the situation. I at least have Allie. If something happened to me and I went missing, she'd search for me. She'd likely call my sister, Ellie, and they'd contact every hospital, morgue, and the local news to track my whereabouts.

To have no one must be absolute loneliness.

I glance at the headset that's charging beside the television. Allie isn't allowed to take it with her for sleepovers. Whenever she plays multiplayer online, she has to be monitored by an adult. House rules. I get the pleasure of watching her game via my phone and hanging out with her in the living room to ensure that she's being smart and safe about the information she gives strangers online.

I trust Allie. It's the other creeps online whom I can't trust.

I give Kona a few extra pets and treats before heading to the restaurant to pick up dinner. I should leave the stranger, *John*, alone. I'm not sure that he even wants my help, but I can't seem to stop myself from grabbing dinner and showing up in front of his door.

With a firm knock, I wait for him to unlock the door and grant me entrance inside.

He pulls open the door and glances me over. "You brought dinner."

"I said I would," I answer, stalking in through the open door and breezing right past him.

"Let yourself in," he says under his breath.

I ignore his remark. He's probably grumpy from a six-week coma. I'm sure I would be too. I waltz into the kitchenette and drop the paper bag filled with dinner on the table. "I wasn't sure what you eat, so I bought quite a few things. Whatever you don't finish, pop in the fridge, and you'll have a meal for tomorrow and the next day."

"You're not staying."

It's not a question, and I can't tell if there's disappointment or relief. He's made it impossible to read his body language or his tone.

"I have to get back to Kona." And while I had intended to join him for dinner, there's something about him, a darkness that swirls around him, that makes me nervous.

"Kona, as in Hawaii?" His brow is tight. "That's a far way from New York City."

"My dog, Kona," I say, and clear my throat.

"Sit." His words are a command as he pulls out an empty chair and nods for me to take it.

I open my mouth to object. I'm not a dog. I don't take verbal commands as orders. "I don't want to overstay my welcome."

"I invited you to sit," he says.

I oblige, if only because I brought dinner and I'm looking forward to the meal in front of me. We sit and eat. There's a stillness over the room. I use the wooden chopsticks while the mysterious man sitting across from me utilizes a fork.

"You didn't mention earlier that you have a pet. What kind of dog do you have?"

"An Australian Shepherd."

"I'd like to meet him or her."

"Her," I say, and reach for my glass of water that he put out on the table. I take a sip, and my gaze is locked on his. "You still don't remember anything from before the shooting?" I ask.

"Nothing." He shifts uncomfortably in his seat and cracks his neck from side to side with a wince.

Why do I feel he may be hiding something from me?

"Well, I've got to call you something. If you can't remember your name, the hospital had you listed as John Doe."

His top lip snarls at his disgust. "That's not my name."

"Obviously," I say, and roll my eyes. "But you need a name, and Bearded Bad Boy just doesn't seem appropriate."

His eyes widen. There's a hint of recognition, and for a man who supposedly doesn't remember anything,

I can't help but wonder if he's been hiding the truth from me or had a memory resurface.

Or it could be that I just gave him a nickname that he finds insulting.

"What did you call me?"

"Bearded Bad Boy," I say, like it's a phrase I just invented.

His gaze is stone as he stares straight into my soul.

I refuse to flinch or cower. He's the one insisting he doesn't know who he is.

"That's an interesting choice."

I take another bite of dinner, glancing at my plate, avoiding his heated stare. What the hell does he remember? It can't be a coincidence, his roughness with my remark. "Yeah, just a name I heard that seems to fit you." I don't elaborate where I *heard* this name.

His jaw is tight, and he reaches for his water glass, taking a small sip. "You think I'm a bad boy?"

I gesture at his arm. "The tattoos are a dead giveaway. Do you remember the significance of any of them?" I want to ask about the star tattoo on his chest, the same one I've seen.

"Do I remember why I have ink on my arms? No," he says. "Just like I can't recall my name. But I'm certain that Bearded Bad Boy isn't it." He takes several more bites of food, but I get the distinct impression that it's to show me that he's done speaking, at least about his name.

Why get into such a frenzy over the nickname? Is it him, and he remembers something shady or sinister from his past?

He finishes eating before I'm done and begins clearing the dishes and putting the uneaten and leftover meals into the fridge. It's like he's telling me it's time for me to finish up and leave without saying a word.

After eating, I clear my dishes and rinse the remaining dishware in the sink before loading the dishwasher. "I should go." It doesn't seem like he wants me hanging around, and I've insulted him, whether intending to or not.

His jaw remains tense as he walks me toward the door. "Thank you for all that you've done. But it isn't necessary."

"I'd say having a roof over your head is necessary. The weather forecast is calling for rain tonight. You're welcome."

He exhales a breathy sigh and opens the door. "I do appreciate all that you've done for me—"

There's a silence that follows. Has he forgotten my name, or is it something else? I opt to remind him of my name. He's been in a coma. I wouldn't fault him for forgetting who I am. "It's Sadie," I say.

"I know. I'd never forget you," he whispers. The roughness dissipates like smoke wafting away and out of an open window.

"Of course not, just yourself," I say, and smile, attempting to make a joke. It's not a great one, and he doesn't laugh.

Probably because it's true and painful. "Where did you come up with your *fun* nickname for me?" He holds the door open, and I stand inside the entryway, waiting to leave. I should bail before I confess the stupidest and most ridiculous reasoning for the little name that I bestowed on him.

"It's ridiculous," I say, stalling. Why does he have to bring it up?

"You didn't just derive it from thin air."

Does he know? Could he be remembering the past? I doubt that if he does, he'll remember any semblance of me. And that's far-reaching for me to think that *Bearded Bad Boy* in the VR world is *him*.

"My niece has a video game she likes to play with other people. One of those gamers is *Bearded Bad Boy*," I say. "You just... the name seemed fitting."

His eyes crinkle with the hint of a smile. "Is that so?"

I point toward the door that remains open. "I should go," I say. He's made it clear that he's asking me to leave, escorting me out the door. Besides, he's a stranger. How much do I know about him? He could be a murderer, and I might be his next target. Getting shot in the forest and being left for dead might be a warning.

"I'll see you around, Sadie."

The way he says my name makes my stomach flutter like I'm in middle school all over again. Except, this time, I'm helping a man I know nothing about. If I told anyone, they'd warn me to steer clear. He's dangerous or, at the very least, involved with men who want him dead.

———

"Sadie!" I waltz into work two days later, and my boss, Connor, gestures for me to join him in his office.

Inwardly, I grimace. My stomach flops, and I'm filled with dread. I drag my feet as I shuffle into his office.

"Close the door," he says.

"Is something wrong, sir?" I ask.

"Care to explain why a guest is staying in one of the rooms marked in our system as unavailable?"

"I don't know what you mean." I keep my hands at my sides and do my best not to fidget or appear guilty. What I did wasn't that bad. There are worse crimes to commit. I helped a guy out. We had an empty room at the hotel.

"You checked a guest into a room that needed repairs. This morning, I had one of our maintenance team inspect the room since you failed to comment on what made the room unavailable. Imagine my surprise when I discovered a guest was occupying that room."

I open my mouth and quickly shut it. "I must have—"

Connor holds out his hand, stopping me from digging my own grave. "I don't know what you're up to, but it was clear the gentleman in question didn't have a room reservation and isn't anywhere within our system. You're fired."

"What?" I gasp. My stomach drops, and my hands tremble at my side. "Sir, I can explain."

"Giving out free rooms to your friends isn't permissible. You ought to know that, Sadie. We don't run a brothel around here."

"Excuse me?" I choke out. He can't be serious. "I can assure you, that isn't what is going on."

"I don't care what reasoning you have for what you did, but as far as I'm concerned, it's theft. You're lucky we're not charging you and just dismissing you from the property. Gather your belongings and get out."

"It was just a mistake," I say, trying to justify the guest in the room marked as unavailable and needing repair.

"Get out," his voice bellows, and a shiver pierces me. I stalk toward the door, my hand on the metal handle. "Unless you want to offer me the same services you offered the gentleman caller last night."

"Excuse me?" Suddenly, getting fired doesn't seem that bad.

"We have cameras, Sadie. You went into his hotel room twice yesterday. You can't tell me it wasn't a bootie call."

"Fuck you." I yank open his office door and stomp out. There's no point in explaining myself to Connor. He's a pig.

I clench my purse in my hand and storm out of the hotel through the front entrance, stalking toward the parking garage.

How dare he insinuate that I'm bringing in clientele for sex and suggest I do the same for him? The nerve of him!

———————

"Thanks for meeting me." The barstool swivels beneath my weight as I order another round.

"Sorry I couldn't get here any sooner." She gestures toward the ring, indicating that her husband is to blame. They've had a rocky start, the first two years married, and I don't see it getting any better for her. Her husband is a narcissistic asshole. I keep telling her to leave his ass. She can stay with Allie and me, but it's not like we have much room. She'd be crashing on the couch.

"I'll have what she's having," Clare says, and grabs the seat beside me, propping herself on it. "What's up?"

"I got fired." I grab the shot and down it in an instant. I've had three drinks already. Or was it four? "Connor is such a bosshole."

Clare already knows I lost my job. I texted her and told her I needed her at the bar with me ASAP.

Allie is spending the night with the neighbor girl, so at least I don't have to worry about her seeing me drunk when I come home.

The bartender pours us each a shot. "To the men who are dicks in our lives," Clare says.

Clare and I clink glasses before throwing them back in unison.

I laugh under my breath. She isn't wrong. "That asshat Connor, I swear if he walks in here, I'd knee him in the groin and then dump a bottle of tequila on him." He disgusts me. I'm not entirely innocent because I hid a stranger in one of the hotel rooms, but it's not like he's a wanted felon. And we weren't having sex. The nerve of him to suggest it!

"That'd be a waste of perfectly good tequila," Clare says. "But I get your point. He doesn't deserve to work at the hotel. Didn't you say he only has the job because his family owns the hotel chain?"

"His brother Levi inherited the Luxenberg. Rumor has it that he felt bad for Connor, so he gave him a management role for one of the New York hotels."

"Well, he should have fired his ass." My blood boils, and I gesture to the bartender again that we want another round.

"Maybe you should slow down," Bearded Bad Boy says as he approaches.

He's in a dark t-shirt and blue jeans that hug him just the right way. My eyes linger longer than they should. Does he notice? "What are you doing here? Are you stalking me?"

He huffs under his breath and leans back against the bar. "No. I was just finishing some business, seeing how I need a new place to crash."

"I'm Clare," my friend says, putting out her hand and introducing herself. She's wearing a huge grin and glances between him and me. "And you are?"

"He's leaving," I say.

"You don't have to," Clare interjects. The girl doesn't know when to keep her mouth shut. "I'm sorry, my friend just had a bad day. Her boss is an asshole, and she got fired from her job."

"He fired you?" Bearded Bad Boy says. I swear that I hear him growl under his breath. His top lip twitches with a snarl. "I'll kill him." He's not quiet with his threat.

And as much as I'd like to see Connor pummeled and taken out of the equation, I don't need anyone sticking up for me or my honor. "That isn't necessary." I hold up my hand to stop him from doing what, I'm not sure. "It was just a dumb job. I can find another one."

"Maybe she can come and work for you," Clare says with a smirk. "And you are?" The girl is persistent. I never told her about the shooting in the forest or the stranger at the hospital. We don't see each other often enough. I shouldn't be calling her to vent as I unravel, but I need someone to help me screw my head back on and make sure I don't fall into bed with some random guy at the bar.

Clare is usually the sensible one, at least when drinking is involved.

"Dmitri."

"You remember your name?" I can't hide the excitement bubbling inside of me. "That's good!"

"I remember some things," he says, not elaborating further.

Clare glances from Dmitri to me. "You forgot who you were?"

"It's a long story," I say, not making Dmitri share it if he doesn't want to with Clare.

She downs the second shot she ordered while the bartender makes another round. "I'll be back. I need to use the ladies' room." Clare shuffles from the bar and slips past Dmitri, leaving the two of us alone.

"I should go with her," I say, and Dmitri's hand falls to my arm.

"Because you have to go, or you don't want to be alone with me?"

I purse my lips and realize that he's right. "I'm not mad if that's what you're wondering."

"So, I was the reason you were fired," Dmitri says. His brow is furrowed, and his hand drops from my arm, balling into fists at his sides. The muscles in his arms twitch, veins bulging as anger seems to ascend to the surface.

"It's nothing," I say, and shrug off the situation. "I should have been looking for another job. Connor, my boss, is a tool. He only has the job because his brother owns the hotel chain."

"Connor must be the short, balding man with bushy eyebrows and ear hair?"

I chuckle, Dmitri winning a smile from me. "I didn't notice the ear hair."

"How could you not notice it?" he asks, wide-eyed. "It was quite repulsive, and I can only imagine that it would flail in the wind outside and perhaps even give him wings."

"Pigs don't have wings."

"You know the adage when pigs fly," Dmitri quips, and reaches for the shot that the bartender brings over, stealing it from me. "You've had enough to drink."

My shoulders slump in defeat. "Fine. Are you going to drive me home when the night is over?" I'm not serious about my request. The man doesn't owe me anything.

"I will take your keys," Dmitri says, his tone firm. He's not playing around. "You're not getting behind the wheel inebriated."

Clare waltzes back from the bathroom and scoots past Dmitri, resuming her position on the barstool. "Thanks for saving my seat. What'd I miss?" She's all smiles, her cheeks rosy and flushed from the two shots that she's had since arriving at the club.

The music pulsates through the small space. "We should dance," Clare says, and slides easily off the barstool. She grabs my arm and pulls me off my seat.

The room sways, and I stumble into Dmitri's arms. Or maybe he steps in the way to stop me from falling. I'm not sure which happens first.

"You can barely stand," Dmitri says.

"Because you won't let me."

He releases his hold on my arms, but his hands are right next to my hips.

"She's okay. I've got her," Clare says, and grabs my arm, dragging me onto the dance floor.

Dmitri watches from between our barstools, his back to the wooden bar top. He folds his arms across his chest. His brow is tight as he watches us dance.

"Do you have a thing for Dmitri?" Clare shouts over the music.

My cheeks burn, and my eyes widen, but he's far enough away that I doubt he can hear her question. At least, I hope he can't.

"What? No," I say a little too quickly. "We're just friends." I'm not sure we're friends, but I helped him out, and he's telling me what I can and can't do tonight. Not that I had any intention of driving home. I was going to take the subway, but still, I don't like being bossed around by anyone.

"Well, he's checking your ass out." Clare grins and offers him a wave to let him know she caught him staring.

"He's probably checking you out," I mutter. Clare always had a talent for catching a man's gaze and keeping his attention.

That isn't me. I'm the girl everyone wants to be friends with, the girl next door. It sucks.

Not that I want to be tied down, but I wouldn't mind settling down with the right man. But that's a fantasy. I have Allie. She takes priority. Men complicate things. Well, rather, relationships complicate matters.

"No, he likes you," Clare says. "You should dance with him."

I groan. "I'm not going to do that."

"And why not?" she asks. The girl cannot take a hint that there are some things I might not want to discuss. "At the very least, bump and grind with him."

"Excuse me?" I laugh at her suggestion.

"Come on. When's the last time you've bedded a man?" She holds up a hand. "You don't have to answer that, but just think about it. You've got a lot of pent-up frustration from today, and he can handle your needs."

Clare waves at him with a wide grin on her face. "She wants to fuck you!" She tries to shout over the music, but I'm grateful he can't hear what she says. Hopefully he can't lip-read, either.

"You are evil." I should be angry at Clare, but I'm not. The girl has my best intentions at heart, usually.

Dmitri struts across the dance floor. His eyes are warm. They crinkle upwards when he smiles subtly. "What was that?" he asks, and whether he understood her words, he's more of a gentleman than most guys.

"Dance with me," I say, and Clare shoves me at Dmitri, her hand on my back, pushing me closer. My arms wrap around his neck, and his hands are at my waist, steadying me as the room spins. Even if I wanted to take him home and invite him into my bed, I doubt anything would happen. There's nothing sexy about taking a drunk woman who can barely stand on her own two feet home.

"It would be my pleasure," Dmitri says, pulling me closer and tight against him. His breath tickles my ear as he leans in to whisper, "Did your friend just tell me that she wants to fuck me?"

I cough and choke on his words. "No," I squeak, half-grateful he misinterpreted her words.

"Okay, good. Because she isn't my type."

"Smart, funny, and gorgeous isn't your type?" I ask, glancing up at him. "That's too bad."

"No, it is, but she's not the one I'm interested in," Dmitri whispers.

I shiver, and he pulls me tighter against him. His hand rests against my lower back, and in soft motions, he's caressing my skin, inching his fingers under the hem of my shirt.

Reaching onto my tiptoes, I pull Dmitri down, wanting to kiss, taste, and devour every ounce of him.

He pulls back and clears his throat. "It's late. You've had more than enough to drink. I should get you home."

"If you're not interested, all you have to do is say as much." I shrug out of his grasp.

Dmitri's eyes tighten, and his jaw is tense. "We should offer Clare a ride home."

He's far more of a gentleman than I would have thought.

"Worried about being alone in the car with me?"

"I'm concerned about leaving your friend at the bar, alone, with dozens of men looking to take advantage of a pretty young woman."

His words burn through me. "If you like her that much, you take her home." I stalk away from him for the bathroom.

The room sways as I walk, and Dmitri spins me around to face him, his hands firm on my shoulders. "Why are you fighting with me?"

"I don't need your pity." I fold my arms across my chest, putting up all barriers around myself and my heart.

"Do you think that's what I'm doing, pitying you? For what? Losing your job?"

I didn't come to the bar tonight to find Dmitri and fight with him. "I'm going home," I say, and shuffle away from him toward Clare.

"Are we leaving?" she asks, glancing at me, seeming to have overheard a little of the conversation. Or she's astute as hell.

"Yes," I say, and grab her arm, linking ours together.

"Subway or cab?" Clare asks.

I didn't drive tonight. I dropped my car off at my apartment and took the subway here. "Subway," I say. "How'd you get here?"

"Same, but I'm taking a cab home."

Dmitri is right behind us, following every step of the way. He opens the door for Clare, and we slide out through the front entrance together. She tosses up an arm, hailing a cab. It takes a minute before one pulls up at the corner.

"Do you want to share a ride?" she asks.

Dmitri steps toward the cab. "I'll get her home safely."

Clare pins me with a silent stare, waiting for my acceptance. "I'll be fine."

"Text me when you get home and have fun," Clare says with a wave, shuffling into the back of the cab. Dmitri shuts the back door for her once she's inside.

"Cab or subway?" he asks.

"I'm taking the subway." I stalk down the sidewalk, and he's right at my hip, like a shadow that won't disappear.

"Me too," Dmitri says. He follows me two blocks and down the stairs.

"I'll be fine." I insist that he doesn't need to accompany me if that's what he's doing.

Maybe I should be concerned that he's following me, but he could quickly head in the opposite direction when we head inside, or he could take a different train.

"Of course you will. How about I walk you home?" His arm falls around my waist, holding me close and tight. For a man who's made it clear that he's not interested in me, I can't help but wonder why he's nestled at my hip.

Is he worried that I'll find someone else to go home with?

Is he trying to claim me as his own?

I head down to the platform, and he's at my side. He can't go back to the hotel without paying for a room. "I don't need a bodyguard."

"Even so, I'd feel more comfortable making sure that you get home."

I glance him over. Tattoos cover his arms and peek out beneath his shirt at his neck. I trip over my feet, and he clutches me against him, keeping me from falling on my face or, worse, onto the train tracks.

"That's it. I'm not taking no for an answer." He's firm in his decision.

I don't argue. My body sways as the train arrives, and he helps me aboard. He stands behind me, one arm around my waist, the other holding the metal bar as we stand on the train.

The doors close, and I nearly fall on my ass. Thankfully, Dmitri is nestled against my bottom, keeping me safe. His hold on me tightens. "Don't ever think for a second that I don't find you attractive, *Malishka*," he whispers. "It takes every ounce of self-control not to bend you over and fuck you right here for everyone to see."

My breath catches in my throat. It's doubtful anyone else heard what he said, but I heard every word, as he intended.

The train is warm as we head past several stops until we reach the destination. "This is it," I say on our approach. "Are you walking me to my front door?"

"That's the plan." He accompanies me off the train and onto the platform as we head for the escalator.

He's at my side. His arm wraps around my hip as he keeps me tightly against him. There's a warmth that he exudes, or perhaps the alcohol that's made me toasty inside, along with his presence.

I guide him back to my apartment. The walk from the subway is a few blocks, and it's late. I don't admit that I'm grateful for the company as I sway on my feet. Dmitri keeps me upright and balanced.

I unlock the main entrance to the apartment complex, and he accompanies me into the elevator. "You don't have to walk me inside. I'm safe now," I say.

"What floor?" he asks as he stands in front of the panel in the elevator.

"Six," I say.

He presses the button for the sixth floor, and after the doors close, I press the buttons for all the other floors above six.

"You're a monster," he jokes.

It's the middle of the night. How many people are riding the elevator at this hour? "I know." I lean into

Dmitri while the elevator ascends, and we reach the sixth floor.

The double doors open, and I shuffle with my purse, digging out my keys while stepping out of the elevator. He's right beside me every step of the way.

Is he waiting for me to invite him inside? I push the key into the lock and turn, grabbing him by the shirt, pulling him hard against me, my lips crashing down on his. Isn't that why he's here?

"Sadie," he whispers, his voice rough and throaty as his lips fall to my neck. There's a heat swirling around, making me want to rip my clothes off within his presence.

I'm stifling, and his lips only further make me melt in the hallway. I reach behind me for the door handle and shuffle inside.

He's right with me, and so is Kona, jumping and barking in excitement at my presence.

Or maybe she's alerting me to the newcomer accompanying me.

"Hello," he grunts as he kicks the door shut with his foot and is shoved back against the front entrance.

Kona has pounced, two paws on his chest, sniffing and deciding if he's worthy of entering. He's momentarily startled, and I can't tell if he likes dogs or despises them. He certainly doesn't appear afraid.

"Kona, down," I say, pointing for her to sit.

She releases her hold on Dmitri and steps back, sitting by the front door, staring at him. Her tail is wagging, the biggest giveaway that she's friendly and not threatening.

I glance at Dmitri over my shoulder as I flip on the lights and wince from the brightness.

He bends down to Kona's level and cuddles my girl, giving her pets. If she were a guard dog, he'd have just broken her.

"You're a dog person," I say, glancing at Dmitri as Kona has taken a liking to him, rubbing up against him for more rubs.

I don't dare admit I'm jealous that she's won his attention tonight. I had momentarily forgotten about Kona and had envisioned him slamming the door shut and fucking me against it.

I suppose that's not about to happen.

Bummer.

"As a child, I had a rescue mutt when we first moved to America."

I'm curious what else he remembers. Have all of his memories returned?

I flip on the kitchen light. "Can I get you a drink?"

Dmitri shakes his head, his eyes on me as he stands and follows me into the kitchen. "No, I'm good."

Kona accompanies us, but she's calmer and relaxed now that she's sniffed out Dmitri and decided he's welcome here.

"Are you—good?" I ask, stepping toward him. I sway slightly, and he reaches out, his hands on my hips, steadying me. I prefer to think of it as embracing me, that he wants me, and this isn't him just being chivalrous. Maybe he feels he has to return the favor after I helped him. Or maybe he wants something, like a place to stay for the night since he got kicked out of the hotel room.

His brow tightens as he stares deep into my gaze. "We should get you into bed. It's well past your bedtime."

"You don't know what time I go to bed."

He nods. "True, but you're falling over on your feet. It's late, and you need rest."

"I'm not drunk," I counter, slipping out of his grasp and stalking out of the kitchen.

His hands grasp my hips from behind. He's warm and strong, nestled up against me. "You've had a lot to drink, *Malishka*."

I stop walking long enough to revel in the feel of his arms wrapped around me. "What's that?" I mumble, curious about the name.

"Lead me to your bedroom. I'm going to tuck you into bed."

I point lazily at the door down the hallway, and he escorts me to the bedroom. "Hallway and kitchen light," I say.

"On it." He releases his grasp and hurries to shut off the other lights while I stumble into bed. I slip off my heels, kicking them to the floor, and climb under the covers. The bed is soft, plush, and perfect as my head hits the pillow.

I don't have a guest room. The second bedroom is Allie's. Even if I did have a spare bedroom, I wouldn't want Dmitri sleeping in there.

"Stay," I whisper.

The room is in absolute darkness, and I can't see Dmitri if he is here. After a moment, he must enter because his footsteps aren't the least bit silent.

"Stay," I repeat, in case he hadn't heard me earlier.

"I don't want to impose."

"Just climb into bed."

"Bossy," he jokes, and I hear his shoes clamber to the floor. The bed dips a minute later, and the sheets rustle as he gets comfortable.

I roll onto my side, brushing against his arm while facing him. I struggle to keep my eyes open and remain awake.

He lies on his back, completely still. He's far more of a gentleman than I thought possible. "Do you like men?" I ask.

"Excuse me?" He chokes on his words.

"You're lying next to me in bed and haven't tried to cop a feel. I can't help but think it's because you're not attracted to me. Do you prefer to keep the company of men?"

A laugh escapes his throat, and the bed dips as he rolls onto his side. My eyes have adjusted to the darkness, and I can make out his features as he stares back at me. "The things I want to do to you are probably illegal in at least ten states. It's late, and you've had too much to drink. Go to sleep, *Malishka*."

My cheeks burn from his words. "I can't." I'm more awake than I should be. It's probably because Dmitri is lying beside me.

He pulls me closer, tighter. I can smell his masculine aroma as it pierces through the room and blinds my senses.

He's all I want.

All I need.

A yearning pulls me toward him, a craving I can no longer deny. My lips crash against his, and this time he's there, rolling me onto my back with no interruptions.

His body is above mine, tangled between sheets and thin veils of fabric that keep us apart.

I'm starving for his touch and to feel him above me. My fingers tug at the blankets, pushing them down and away. Gently, I stroke the skin of his lower back, inching his boxers down and off as he raises his hips for me.

He's not wearing a shirt, and his chest is bare, warm, perfect.

"Lift your hips," he commands as he shimmies my panties down with my pants in one swoop. I didn't bother to change into pajamas. His hand caresses back up my body, grazing my torso, sliding beneath my shirt as he cups one of my breasts.

Dmitri's lips fall back on mine, hungrily feeding off me as if I'm his life force for survival. We tangle and roll. The sheets twist as I push him down onto his back, taking the lead. I straddle his frame and lift my shirt up and over my head.

His eyes shine up at me while his fingers work the clasp on my purple lace bra. He pinches the clasp. The material falls down my shoulders, and I let it tumble to the floor in a heap with my shirt.

I lean down, my lips brushing against his. Every second is teasing and agonizing, wanting to feel him inside me as I tease him. My insides throb and pulsate. It's pleasurable torture.

Dmitri forcefully rolls us around, pinning me under his weight. "Do you like teasing me?" he asks with a roughness that makes my toes curl and my insides ache, craving more with him.

"I do," I confess, staring up at him, grinning as he grabs my arms, pinning them above my head, dominating every inch of me. A moan spills past my lips, and my hips grind upwards into his.

"I'll bet you want to feel my cock inside your tight little pussy."

"Yes, please." I'm not above begging. My insides throb, and my fingers tremble as I clench onto his hands.

He teases me in return, inching the tip of his cock inside of my pussy. "You like that, baby girl, don't you?"

His words are my undoing. I lift my hips, wanting him to slam his cock inside of me. "Dmitri," I rasp. He binds my hands, and his fingers interlock with mine. It requires too much energy to say anything else. He's the only one who can satisfy the building need burning within me.

I moan and wrap my legs around him, bringing him deeper. His lips cover mine, and I push my tongue inside his mouth. Needy and starving for him.

Each thrust grows more intense.

Primal.

Setting my world on fire.

My heart pounds rapidly against my chest, slamming against my ribcage, trying to break free. "Come for me, *Malishka*," he whispers into my ear, tugging the lobe between his teeth as I tinker on the edge of oblivion.

His words are enough to bring me crashing down like a rollercoaster at full speed, the rush of adrenaline and arousal tingling through every inch of my body. My insides clench, pulsating and trembling as I chase my orgasm, squeezing him tight and holding him against me.

FOUR

DMITRI

The darkness has yet to turn to daylight. Sadie is sound asleep, as is Kona, for which I'm grateful. I don't want the beast startled awake.

After a few minutes of slumber, I sneak out of bed and pull on my boxers and t-shirt. I stumble in the dark, careful not to trip over anything or Kona as she wanders into the bedroom.

It seems I've wakened her, but at least she's not whimpering to go out or waking Sadie. Satisfied that I'm not here to entertain her, she settles onto the floor beside the bed and falls asleep.

Quietly, I sneak out of the bedroom, closing the door, careful not to make a sound. I don't know whether Sadie is a light sleeper or not, but I don't intend to find out.

With the door shut, I flip on a table lamp and glance around the apartment. It's small and quaint. Everything is relatively clean and tidy.

She had mentioned *Bearded Bad Boy*, my handle in the VR world. She must have a headset lying around her apartment.

I spoke with dozens of associates and low-level thugs in the VR world, but no one I did business with was female. Which begs the question, who the hell is Sadie? And how did she happen to stumble onto me during a run in the forest?

I don't believe in coincidences.

If Sadie works for Mikhail, I'd be dead already. But perhaps she's been ordered to keep close tabs on me. And if that's the case, then who hired her?

Wincing, none of it makes sense. Mikhail doesn't hire women to do his bidding. They're too soft, vulnerable, and unreliable.

I touch the scar on my head, grimacing. It no longer hurts, except for the betrayal that burns through me.

My family, the bratva, betrayed me.

Had it been Nikita who wanted me dead? Mikhail? Or had Anton and Savannah been responsible for shooting me and leaving me to die? That doesn't include the countless enemies I've made as a member of the bratva.

I search quietly through her apartment, glancing through the small space until I notice that plugged in beside the television is a VR headset. I slide the headset on and use the controllers to view the settings, finding the account name of the user currently logged into the system. I don't recognize the screen name, *AllieInWonderland*.

I never conversed or played with *AllieInWonderland*.

How the hell does she know who I am?

It's impossible to tell how new her account is based solely on her screen name. She has a handful of games downloaded. The most recently played is Orc Hunter.

I click on the app, open the program, and turn the volume down so as not to wake her or Kona.

I glance through her game settings. She's a level twelve.

Amateur.

It may be a new headset. But why acquire a new account too?

I sign out of her account, loading mine. Mikhail had me use the VR system, as it is a completely untraceable chat interface.

Mikhail never knew my handle. It wasn't necessary since I was tasked with handling the associates. I log into the account. It's considerably early to be signing on. A few months ago, I would have been working at the club until closing. It feels like just a few days ago for me.

Word must have traveled to the associates; they should expect I'm dead. How will they handle seeing a ghost?

There's no one I recognize online, and that doesn't help my situation. I need money and a weapon for protection. I sign out of the headset, not wanting

Sadie to know who I am, although it seems she already has figured me out.

I can't determine how. It's like she knows me without knowing anything about me.

There was one woman who I conversed with online, and she didn't even have her own account. She used her niece's for the better part of a month.

Could it be *her*?

I never got her name. Only that she resides in New York, which doesn't narrow it down much. She sounded hot over the microphone, but I never got a glimpse at her.

I place the headset back where I found it and plug the cord back in, not wanting it to look tampered with, although she's bound to discover that she's been signed out. If I'm lucky, she'll think it's just a glitch from an update.

Her keys are near the door, along with her purse. Abandoned.

I stand, heading for the door, when it swings wide open.

A young girl, all of five feet, stares back at me. "Are you my mom's boyfriend?" she asks.

"Your mom's boyfriend?" I repeat, dumbfounded. Sadie didn't mention that she had a kid. "Yeah, I was just leaving."

She smirks and chews her bottom lip. I swear I've seen Sadie do the exact same thing. "You don't have to leave on my account." She shuts the door behind herself and drops her purse beside Sadie's. "Mom never mentioned you." The kid glances me over, a wide grin on her face.

I run a hand through my hair. "I should go," I say. I'm not particularly bad at lying, but I don't need to ruin this young girl's future or her mother's. The shit I'm wrapped up in is too dangerous for them.

"I'm Allie, by the way." She holds out her hand. The girl has more manners than most men twice her age.

"Nice to meet you, Allie. I'm Dmitri."

"How long have you been dating my mom?" Allie asks.

There's no way in hell I'm about to answer her question or any others she decides to throw at me.

"It's late. Shouldn't you be in bed already?" I can't imagine the girl is old enough to drive. How the hell did she get home?

"Can't sleep," Allie says, and plops herself down on the sofa. The girl is wide awake with bright blue eyes. "Besides, my friend down the hall was being a total brat, TBH."

"TBH?"

"To be honest," Allie says. "She's emo, and I can't stand her." The brunette rolls her bright blue eyes and pulls her knees on the couch. "Are you why mom sent me to that loser's house? She wanted to see her secret boyfriend?"

Allie is going to hate me. No doubt this kid will want nothing to do with me when she finds out that her mother was fired from her job, and I'm the reason behind it. It's for the best. I should leave Sadie and Allie alone.

"We just happened to run into each other. We didn't plan anything for tonight," I say.

Her eyes narrow, and she nods slowly like she's listening but not believing a word coming from my lips.

She's not the only one.

This boyfriend crap is too much, even for me. I don't do girlfriends. I don't have relationships. I steer clear of anything that involves handholding and dates.

I prefer a good fuck and then going home after. What I was trying to do with Sadie when Allie rammed in through the front door.

I clear my throat. "It was nice meeting you, Allie." I grab the door handle, yanking it open.

"You're seriously leaving? That's a dick move."

I doubt her mom would be okay with her using that type of language. "You should head to bed," I say.

"You're not my father."

No, she's right. I'm not her father. I'm not even dating Sadie. We just slept together, and I was trying to sneak out when I got caught by the bright-blue-eyed teenager who likes to ask a thousand and one questions.

Next time, I fuck a girl at a hotel or in her car. I can't deal with this drama.

"Night, Allie," I say, and head out the front door.

That might have been uncomfortable, but at least it wasn't her husband who came through the front door. I've been there, in bed with a woman, and it wasn't a fun night. That's one memory I'd like to squash.

I head for the subway. I need to get across town near the bar. I want to see if Nikita is working.

I need to see if he's alive.

I have a few dollars that I managed to pickpocket the previous night. I had snuck out after dark from the hotel, secured a few wallets from unsuspecting tourists, and then returned to my room. It gave me enough money to cover the subway fare, food, and incidentals until I figure out what the hell I'm doing next.

I had tossed the wallets in the garbage, credit cards included. Had I known that asshole planned to kick me out of the free hotel room, I'd have used one of the stolen credit cards to secure a new booking.

It's dark, and the streets are bare. The trains run all night, and the station nearest her apartment arrives just as I approach the platform. I don't have any great plan. I tend to work on instinct.

I keep an eye on the time, making sure that I arrive before closing. I don't want Nikita or anyone else who works for the bratva to spot me.

After the short subway ride, I walk several blocks to the club, hiding in the darkened shadows of night. I watch outside, near the back entrance where Nikita always leaves from. He may be at home with Lucy and their son, Zion. It's just as likely he's inside until closing, especially with two less employees, Anton and myself.

Did they hire replacements for us? Are we dispensable to Mikhail?

It's nearly two in the morning, the club is winding down, patrons are leaving, and the parking lot grows empty except for the bratva-owned SUV.

Nikita or any other number of Mikhail's men could be driving it. Many of us have access to the vehicles registered to his illegal enterprise.

I hide, remaining out of sight as the last person leaves the club. His suit is crisp, with the keys in his hand as he locks the door.

Nikita Ivanov.

One of my brothers. I don't know where we stand anymore. Hell, I was left for dead. Did no one think to check the hospital? I find the entire ordeal unsettling.

My hands ball into fists as I stalk across the empty parking lot, blocking the SUV's driver's side door.

"Is it really you?" Nikita laughs and coughs, surprise evident in his tone. But I can't tell if it's because he wants me dead and I've disappointed him, or he's genuinely shocked that I'm standing in front of him.

"No, I'm a ghost," I say.

He cracks a wry grin and throws an arm out for a hug. "I thought you were dead, man." Nikita takes a step back and fusses with his hair. He's nervous. I've been around him long enough to catch his tics. What's he hiding?

"Yeah, I'll bet you did." I exhale a heavy breath. I glance him over. He doesn't look worse for wear, but I don't know what he's been through since that afternoon when I was shot.

My memory is foggy for that particular day, but everything leading up to it is crisp and clear. "What the hell happened with Anton and Savannah?"

He runs a hand through his hair again. His suit coat, perfect from afar, has a few wrinkles up close. It's late, and his eyes are worn. It's obvious he's tired, and I caught him off guard.

Good. I prefer to have the advantage, which won't last for long. When he returns to the compound, he'll alert Mikhail that I'm alive.

"Fuck, that was what—six weeks ago?" He shuffles his feet. There's a heaviness between us that looms and hangs overhead. "Anton shot you and then shot me."

"That's a nice story," I say, not believing him. "Why the hell would he shoot you and then leave me in the forest to die?"

"He wanted to take me as a hostage. I was still alive," Nikita says. His voice is firm and unwavering as he meets my stare.

"News flash, so was I."

"I noticed," Nikita says. His jaw twitches. "Where the hell have you been?"

FIVE

SADIE

The bed is cold and empty. Did Dmitri decide to bail last night now that he remembers the past?

Is he married?

Engaged?

I should have asked before falling into bed with him. But damn, it was good. It's been a long time since a man worshipped my body in the way that Dmitri had. Too long.

"Mom?" Allie knocks promptly but doesn't burst through my door like usual.

"Just a sec!" I hurry to grab pajamas from the dresser and put them on in record speed. The bedroom door is unlocked, but she waits patiently. More so than usual. Why is that?

When I'm dressed, I stalk for the door and yank open the handle. "You're home early."

There's a knowing smirk adorning her lips. "I met your boyfriend."

"What?" I cough and clear my throat, my eyes wide.

Shit.

"Did Dmitri just leave?" I ask, brushing past her for the kitchen. I need coffee.

"The hot Russian with a killer body? He left last night."

"Last night," I repeat, confused. "You came home last night? What happened with your friend?" I ask, steering the conversation away from Dmitri. He's not my boyfriend. I don't want Allie getting any crazy ideas.

"We got into a fight because she was being a brat. She wanted to sneak out and visit her boyfriend.

And insisted that I had to cover for her. She left me to babysit her two siblings."

"That's not very nice of her."

"Don't worry, Mom. I ratted her out the minute she left. I called her mother, and she came home. She's probably grounded for the rest of her life!" She pumps her fist into the air as a sign of victory.

"Why wasn't her mother at home?" I ask.

"Hot date?" Allie shrugs. "Your date went well. How long have you been dating Dmitri?"

"We're not, I mean, we're just friends." I don't want my daughter thinking that I screw men I barely know. What happened between Dmitri and me was not typical for me.

I don't do one-night stands.

I've always insisted on putting Allie first. Which means dating has been pushed to the back burner. She'll be off to college in a few years, and I won't have to worry about her.

"Right, friends with benefits," she snickers.

"Allie!" I warn. "That's enough."

"It's not, Mom. You kept your boyfriend from me."

I glare at her.

"Fine, your friend. When can I meet him properly? Like over dinner?"

The girl is persistent. That's one hundred percent me where she gets that. I only have myself to blame for her stubbornness.

"I will see if he's available this weekend." The thought of going out on a date with Dmitri and my daughter makes my stomach tumble. I am not ready for this, but telling her I slept with a man I barely know, that's worse.

I can pull off a fake date if Dmitri is willing to go along. The way I see it, he owes me for helping him, and I lost my job over it.

Not that I blame him, I don't. It was entirely my decision, but the least he can do is help.

But how am I going to get ahold of Dmitri? I don't know where he's staying, living, or working. He doesn't have a cell phone or wallet, for that matter. However, he did manage to pay his fare for the subway.

I hadn't thought anything of it at the moment, but now I'm even more confused.

"Can I go to the mall with Brooke this afternoon?" Allie asks.

"Yes," I say, and grab my purse, fishing out a twenty. "Don't spend it all in one place."

She rolls her eyes. "This will barely buy lunch."

"You're welcome."

————

After dealing with my sassy daughter, I slip on some running clothes and shoes and head out the door.

Dmitri is at the bottom of the porch steps. "How long have you been out here?" I ask.

He sips his coffee, his expression blank. "A while. I'd have bought you a cup, but I wasn't expecting you."

"Waiting for another hot date?" I joke.

His brow furrows. "No." He shuffles his feet, and his eyes remain locked on mine. "You didn't mention that you had a daughter."

"It didn't exactly come up," I say. "We're not dating."

He finishes his coffee and tosses it into the garbage bin nearby.

"I'm going for a run." I point in the direction that I intend to head. "You can join me if you're up for it. I can't promise that you can keep up with me."

"That sounds like a challenge," he rasps.

I start with a nice slow pace, warming up, and Dmitri is beside me. "Cute kid. Single parent?" he asks.

"Yeah, her biological father isn't in the picture." I glance at him before returning my attention to the sidewalk as I head for the nearest park, a little more than two miles away. "What about you? Any kids or a wife I should know about?" I ask.

I'm surprised that he returned to my porch and my apartment after regaining his memories. Why not go home?

"I'm single," Dmitri says, and offers a smile. "I don't usually get tied down."

I laugh under my breath. "You make it sound like commitment is a bad thing."

"It's just not for me," Dmitri says, clarifying his position.

"Don't worry. I wasn't going to propose. It was just one night," I say. One fabulous earth-shattering night, but I can handle being celibate again. It's not like I haven't had plenty of practice over the years.

He jogs beside me in stride, our feet hitting the pavement in unison. "Where'd you go last night?" I ask. It's none of my business, but I still ask, wanting to know where he disappeared. If he'd gone home, he hadn't changed clothes.

"I used to work in a nightclub. I went back to see if one of my colleagues knew anything about the shooting."

"And?"

"Nothing," Dmitri says.

There's a heaviness in the air, and while I don't know him very well, I can't help but wonder if he's lying to me. But why would he lie? What would he gain from it?

"Did you go home?"

"I did not," he says, but doesn't further elaborate. He jogs faster. It's more of a sprint as I work to catch up to him.

If he doesn't want to talk about it, I won't push the issue for now. But he can't stay with me again, not with Allie in the next room.

"So, I need a favor," I say, glancing at him.

"Here we go," he mutters. I jog into the park; the trees canopy over the path, making it much more comfortable than the sun beating down on us.

"Allie, my daughter, has never met any of my boyfriends." I leave off the part that I have had no boyfriends, no relationship, no conquests with men since she was born. It's too embarrassing to talk about. He'll probably think I should have been a nun or something.

"Why is that?" Dmitri asks.

"I don't want to parade men around the house, bring them into her life when they're not going to stick around."

"Fair enough." He slows his pace, and I do the same to stay alongside him. "What's the ask?"

"You two met last night, and she thinks you're my boyfriend. I couldn't tell her otherwise."

"Because you don't want her to think less of you?" Dmitri guesses.

"I don't want her thinking that casual sex is okay. She's thirteen, young, and impressionable. She asked to meet my boyfriend and wants to come out on a date with us."

"Boyfriend?" His voice catches in his throat.

"I know, it's a big request. She thinks we're dating, and I don't want to confuse her, but if it's too much, I can tell her that we broke up—"

"No, I'll do it," Dmitri says, interrupting me before I can ramble further.

"Are you sure?"

"You saved my life. It's the least I can do. What'd you tell her about us?" Dmitri slows, and I do the same.

Maybe he shouldn't be running several miles. He was just in a coma. "There's a bench not too far. We can walk over and sit for a while if you want."

"Sounds good."

We head for the bench, and I brush up against him unintentionally as we walk together. "I haven't told Allie much, although she's likely to ask how we met and how long we've known each other."

His hand falls to my lower back, and I inhale sharply, remembering his body tangled up with mine last night.

"How about we start with the truth?"

His suggestion makes the most sense, but I don't want Allie to think I brought home a guy I barely know.

"She's not ready to hear that I found you with a gunshot wound to your head," I say. Allie is tough and strong, but I don't want to worry her. "How about a compromise? I tell her the truth that I met you while she was at summer camp. And if she asks us during the date, you can ask her all about camp and turn the conversation on her."

The corners of his lips curl upwards. "I'm betting you've done this before."

Does he think that I've slept with lots of men and had to hide them from my daughter? "No, this is the first time." I don't elaborate. It's embarrassing enough to think about. I don't want him poking fun of me next.

He grabs a seat on the wooden bench, and I sit beside him. Already, I miss the warmth of his touch on my lower back. I refrain from scooting closer and leaning against him. We're not an item.

He's doing me this favor to help me because I saved his life.

"Relax, it'll be fine," Dmitri says.

"You've been around teenagers before?"

He clears his throat. "Not really, but I'm sure I can handle whatever questions your daughter tosses at us."

Dmitri has no idea what he's in for when it comes to Allie. "Okay, good," I say, and force a smile.

He stretches his arms and rests them against the back of the bench. He's quiet, brooding, and I can't help but wonder what's going through his mind.

The silence tingles over me like a cool breeze. Dmitri's fingers graze my shoulder and then my hair. His eyes study me as I glance at the trees dead ahead, the forest, everywhere but his steady gaze.

It's too much to meet his stare. He's too intense, and I'm not ready for that. This is all just pretend, but I don't want to admit I enjoyed last night a lot.

I lean back, his fingers strong, warm, and his grip dominant as he shifts closer and tugs a fistful of my hair to lean my face upwards to meet his stare.

"Before last night, when was the last time you were with a man?" Dmitri asks.

I inhale a sharp breath. "Was it that obvious?" I gasp. The air is hot and stifling, and I want to drown myself in the nearest pool of water. Hell, even a puddle would suffice.

"Answer me, *Malishka*." His gaze is steady and unflinching as he stares at me, waiting for my response.

"It's been a while," I whisper. I don't want to be ashamed that I've put my daughter first, but he'll think I'm crazy if I admit how long it's been. Too long is a better answer. It's vague and more than accurate.

"Months?" he asks, his voice low and raspy.

I shift slightly, but it's more of me squirming under his scrutiny while he holds my head in place. He takes control, demands it, and I can't ever remember any man I slept with acting in such a manner.

Dare I say it's hot and highly arousing. Or maybe it's just that he unleashed the sleeping beast inside of me.

"Longer?" he asks.

He won't let the question go.

"Yes, but it's not a big deal. I put my focus and priority on my daughter."

"Last night was different." Dmitri isn't accusatory. He's just pointing out the facts. His hold on me loosens as he plays with my hair. The gesture soothes my racing heart.

"Last night, she wasn't supposed to be home. I had her spend the night down the hall with a friend, but that was my mistake." My cheeks burn just thinking about what it must have been like when Dmitri met Allie. "Was it awkward?"

"What?"

"Running into her." I hadn't warned him I had a daughter because I didn't think he'd ever meet her. Sleeping with him wasn't part of the plan, and I tend to be overly organized.

Dmitri's lips curve upwards. "It was a surprise, but I think I pulled it off pretty well since she thinks we're dating."

SIX

DMITRI

I convince Sadie to let me pick the restaurant, make reservations, and pick the girls up for a dinner date on Saturday night. I'm not sure why I'm nervous. It's not like it's a real date. We're just friends.

My feelings for her can't be real.

She saved me, and I'm sure whatever emotions I feel are mixed up in that and the fact that she's a good person. Sadie tried to give me a place to stay, food, and clothes and probably would have done more if she hadn't been fired, and I confessed that my memory had suddenly returned.

Lying to her was difficult initially, pretending not to know who I was. I'm still lying, keeping secrets. She can't know that I'm bratva, well, used to be bratva. I'm not sure what I am anymore, but there's no leaving the Russian criminal organization. It's a life sentence, for better or worse.

And I see no choice but to entrench myself in their dealings. If Mikhail were responsible for ordering my alleged death, he'd put a hit out on me the first moment he gets.

The club opens in a couple of hours, but undoubtedly, someone is doing the books now that Anton is no longer around. Where did he and Savannah disappear to?

"Surprised to see you back so soon," Nikita says as I enter the club.

The girls haven't come in yet. It's early for them to get ready. The place is empty except for a handful of associates in the basement counting the money laundered through the club.

"Is my job still available?"

"Of course," Nikita says, and frowns. "Why wouldn't it be?"

"It's been a minute since I've been in this place."

"A coma will do that to a guy," Nikita says. He nods for me to follow him to his office, and I oblige. He shuts the door behind us, giving us privacy. "When are you coming back to the compound?"

"Tonight." I can't stay with Sadie again. Being around her puts her life and her daughter's in danger. I shouldn't have promised to take her out Saturday night, but I can't disappoint her, either.

"Good. We've missed you, bro."

"Listen, I'm not sure how quickly you want me to start back at the club, but I need Saturday off."

Nikita folds his arms across his chest. "That's one of our busiest nights." He's waiting for me to elaborate.

"I wouldn't ask if it wasn't essential."

"Are you just going to leave me hanging?" Nikita asks, wanting to know why I need off. It's an unusual request. We have no secrets, but I'm not ready to tell him about Sadie. Besides, there's not anything happening.

"Apparently," I say with a wry smirk. "Consider it a favor for getting shot and being left for dead."

He smiles and shakes his head. "Funny. I'll make sure you have Saturday off, but don't make this a habit."

———————

After leaving the bar, there's little choice but to face the past and return to the compound. If I don't, Nikita is bound to tell Mikhail, the leader of the bratva, that I'm alive.

He should hear it from me.

Am I nervous? I'd be crazy not to be concerned, but I can't stay in New York without facing Mikhail and his men.

And I'm not a man to run and hide.

I've acquired a gun, not by any legal methods, but I'm packing heat in case things go south. I'm prepared. And the more I've stewed over what happened, I don't believe Mikhail set out a hit on me.

Nikita and I had been the ones ordered to kill Savannah and Anton.

We failed.

Mikhail might be pissed about that, but it has to be them if he's after anyone.

I take the subway across town and then grab a ride-share service. I have them drop me off a couple of blocks from the compound.

The weather is nice, excellent for a summer's day. I walk the last couple of blocks until I reach the guard gate. Ivan is on watch, and his jaw drops when he looks at me.

"Shit, I've seen a ghost," Ivan says, and rubs his eyes before stepping out of the booth. "Where the hell have you been?"

"Left for dead," I say. My mouth is dry, and my heart pounds against my ribcage. Maybe I should devise another plan, a different story, to keep Sadie out of this mess. Won't Mikhail ask where I've been? He'll have questions.

Ivan stares at me, dumbfounded, before shaking the mental cobwebs away. "Mikhail is going to shit himself," Ivan says.

I crack a wry grin. "That'd be a sight to see."

Ivan glances me over, convinced I'm not a harm to the family. After all, I am one of them. He opens the gate, allowing me to enter.

"Do me a favor and don't call the house. I'd like to surprise Mikhail."

"Fuck, are you trying to get me fired?" Ivan asks with a nervous laugh. Sweat drips from his forehead.

Why the hell is he so nervous? My stomach is somersaulting. I'm glad I haven't eaten much today.

"Won't be much of a surprise if you announce I'm home," I say.

"Fair enough." Ivan watches me as I stalk across the stone driveway and up the front steps. While I don't have my key, the door's lock offers a fingerprint reader installed within the past year.

I lift my hand, my right index finger against the reader, and it clicks into the unlocked position. I open the door, and fresh paint and cleaner smell burn my nostrils.

What mess was cleaned up this week?

My footsteps aren't invisible. I'm not the least bit quiet, nor do I try to be as I glance around the compound. Children's voices carry into the hallway from the playroom, along with laughter.

Madisyn and Lucy are chatting, but I can't quite distinguish about what, not that it matters. I'm not here to eavesdrop.

I approach Mikhail's office, but it's empty.

He could be anywhere. But I assume he's home, or Ivan would have said otherwise.

"We need to hire a nanny," Mikhail's voice trails from the playroom.

"And we would if you liked any of the prospects we've interviewed," Madisyn says.

I step toward the open door, standing guard outside the room, watching the two lovebirds interact.

"Dmitri!" Mikhail's eyes light up, and a smile grazes his features. I can't tell if it's because I've saved him from whatever conversation he was involved in with Madisyn or if he's relieved that I'm alive.

"I'm back," I say with a forced smile. "Miss me?"

"We thought you were dead." Lucy's voice is soft and fragile. Her brow is pinched, and she bites down on her bottom lip like she's trying not to cry.

Shit.

I was never that close with any of the ladies, but that doesn't mean my supposed death didn't hit hard for them.

"Yeah, funny story." I don't even graze a smile. "I was left for dead, brought into the hospital as a John Doe, and in a coma for several weeks."

"Wow," Lucy whispers, her mouth open and eyes wide.

Madisyn smacks Mikhail's arm. "I told you!" she scolds him. "No body, no funeral. But you don't listen to me."

"You had a funeral for me?" I shift on my feet, uncomfortable at the ends that Mikhail went to when I was supposedly dead.

What the hell did they bury if I wasn't in the casket?

"It was just a small service," Mikhail says, and waves the air dismissively. "Enough about that grave mistake. You're back and look awfully good for a dead man." He gestures for me to follow him to his office.

It's probably for the best. The children don't need to hear what I've been through.

"I had several weeks of sleep," I say.

"I'll bet," Mikhail mutters. "We had our men comb the woods, but no one recovered a body. I guess that's because someone else found you first." He closes the door to his office after I've joined him, giving us some privacy.

"Any word on Anton or Savannah?" I ask.

"Nothing." He sits at the edge of his desk. "Any idea where they might have gone?"

"No. They left my ass for dead. I can't say I know where they disappeared to."

Mikhail's eyes flicker. "Do you suspect Nikita's involvement?" he asks.

I shake my head. I'm not selling him out when he may not be to blame. "I just find it peculiar that I was left in the forest to die, and Nikita returned home."

"Nikita was brought to the hospital, dropped off. He swears he doesn't remember getting there and doesn't know where Anton disappeared to with Savannah."

It doesn't add up. "And no one asked about any other gunshot patients brought in?" I ask.

Mikhail's jaw is tight, his hands bunched into fists at his side. "We were trying to mitigate the damage. Police were crawling all over Nikita's hospital room. I imagine they did the same to yours."

"So, you knew I was alive?"

"I heard a John Doe was brought in, and they didn't think he'd make it. I assumed it was you until I saw a dark-haired girl speak to the doctor. At that point, I thought the patient was no longer a John Doe."

"And you didn't go looking for me?"

"I had a half dozen men search the forest, but by the time Nikita could tell us what happened, the evidence had washed away with the rain, and you weren't anywhere to be seen."

I'm not bitter about it. Mikhail did what he thought was right. It was a tough decision, and we must live with the consequences.

We lost Anton that day.

Even if he's not dead, he's cut off from the family.

"You look good for a dead man," Mikhail says, pushing himself off the desk. He grabs a bottle of whiskey from the cabinet. "Do you want a drink?"

Never turn down an offer from the pakhan, alcohol included. "Sure," I say.

He pours us each a glass and takes the first sip. I follow suit, not that I thought he'd poison me. If he wanted me dead, he'd have already put a bullet into my head.

"Where have you been staying?" Mikhail asks, swirling the amber liquid around before taking a swig.

"Aside from the hospital? With a new friend." I don't elaborate.

"Does she have a name?" Mikhail asks. He never lets anything go.

I hadn't planned on mentioning her. There wasn't any reason to bring her up. "Sadie," I say, glancing down at the amber liquid. I lift the glass to my lips and swallow all of it at once.

"Sadie," Mikhail repeats. "Are you fucking her? Because Hannah and Luka are getting married in a month, and your hot little piece of ass could be the perfect explanation for where you've been."

Leave it to Mikhail to find a way to cover his ass.

I sit at his words, falling into the leather chair opposite his desk. "What are you suggesting?" I don't like how Mikhail's mind works, suggesting that I lie to my bratva brothers.

"Bring her to the wedding, parade her around. And when the others ask, and they inevitably will, you'll tell them that you've been staying with her. You two are an item or whatever you want to fake."

I can't believe that I'm hearing Mikhail correctly. "You want me to bring Sadie here under false pretenses?"

"Not here," he says, gesturing to his office and surroundings. "But in general, yes. I want her to attend the wedding, at least one dinner prior, and perhaps lunch with the girls. Because let's face it, if you only bring her to the wedding, no one will believe that the two of you are serious."

———

It's been three days since I've seen Sadie. I still feel awful about her losing her job. I have two options, show up at the hotel and threaten the manager who fired her ass or give her a job where I work. The second option is a bit more challenging because it involves working for the bratva. And while I don't want to involve her in my messes, it's a little too late.

As it is, I haven't told her I need her to be my fake girlfriend for a bratva wedding.

Baby steps.

The last time I saw Sadie before we departed our separate ways, I had her jot down her phone number. I've since gotten a cell phone and texted her the time that I'd pick her up. I often text her an emoji, or she sends me a silly picture.

Just last night, she asked me if I liked the color, Sassy Sangria, that she painted her toenails. It was very pink, but the girl could pull anything off and look stunning. And I never had a fetish for feet, but damn, hers are hot.

We may be pretending to be in a relationship, but it would seem strange from Allie's point of view if we weren't communicating.

I head on up the stairs to her apartment and press the buzzer. With the flowers in one hand, I wait for her to let me inside the building. I head up to her floor, and she already has the front door ajar.

"Sadie?" I knock as it inches open.

"Come in," she calls from inside the apartment.

Allie is sitting on the couch, pinning me with her gaze. She glances me up and down, stands, and approaches me. "Are the flowers for me?" she asks smugly.

I hand her a tiny bouquet pressed against the larger one for Sadie. "These are for you."

She rolls her lips together. I surprised her. "Thanks." She takes the mixed bouquet of colorful daisies and brings them into the kitchen. "Mom!" Allie shouts across the apartment. "Where are the vases?"

"Above the refrigerator in the cabinet," Sadie says, but she doesn't shout. She rounds the corner to the kitchen wearing the cutest and sexiest but modest black dress I've ever seen. It hugs her breasts, but it covers her, leaving my imagination to determine whether she's wearing a bra and what it might look like beneath the dress.

Satin?

Lace?

I prefer to think she's not wearing any undergarments.

Her skirt flows outward and stops just above her knees.

With her back to the living room, she leans on the sofa for support while she slips on her heels.

What I wouldn't give to be that couch right now, nestled up against her warm body.

I clear my throat and offer to help Allie since I'm a good foot taller than her. "Here, let me." I reach for the cabinet above the refrigerator. There are bottles of alcohol along with a clear crystal vase.

"What about for my flowers?" Allie whines. "I can't share Mom's vase. Do we have another?" Her gaze is set on Sadie.

Sadie slips her heels on. "You brought her flowers?" There's a smile adorning her face, and her cheeks are rosy. I can't determine if it's her makeup or she's blushing.

"I brought you both flowers." I show her the bouquet in my hand that's for her.

"They're beautiful," Sadie says, admiring the bouquet. "You've found the vase. Can you put them in the water while I dig out something for Allie's flowers?"

Allie opens the top drawer and hands me a pair of scissors. I run the sink and cut the stems under the running water before filling the crystal container with water and placing Sadie's flowers into the vase.

Sadie opens the bottom cabinet under the sink and grabs an empty glass bottle. She hands the empty container to Allie. "Here, use this."

"That's cringy, Mom."

Sadie laughs under her breath, and her cheeks burn even more. It's not her makeup causing her skin to heat up. "So is your attitude."

"Burn," Allie says. She snatches the glass bottle and cuts the stems down to force the flowers to fit.

Sadie mouths *sorry* to me. I'd bet anything that Sadie was probably like Allie as a kid.

Defiant.

Independent.

And doesn't take shit from anyone.

"Are you ladies ready for dinner?" I ask.

Allie heads out of the apartment and to the elevator. She hits the button, waiting for the elevator to arrive, while Sadie locks the door. I wait beside Sadie, my hand falling to the small of her back, keeping her close.

"Thanks," she whispers.

I don't ask what for. The ruse isn't up yet. We have an entire night to get through, and it's not like we have anything planned. We've texted a few times but nothing substantial.

The place is within walking distance of her apartment, a couple of blocks north. Once we head out of the building, Allie strides ahead while I slip my hand in Sadie's. "Is this okay?" I ask.

"Yes," she says with a shy smile. "But she's in front of us."

"I'm sure she'll turn around at some point," I counter. "We have to make it look convincing that we're together."

Sadie tugs her bottom lip between her teeth.

"What is it?" I ask.

"It's been a long time since I've dated anyone."

"Pretend dated," I whisper, reminding her this is all a game to keep Allie from knowing the truth.

Which is what, exactly? That Sadie brought me home, and we slept together? There's no crime in that, and I'd know, considering the number of felonies I've committed.

What we didn't wasn't even illegal in most states. I've had kinkier sex. Not that it was boring by any means, but it was vanilla. Very delicious and addictive vanilla. What I wouldn't give to lick actual vanilla ice cream off—

Sadie snaps her fingers in my face. "Dmitri, did you hear a word I said?"

Shit.

"Sorry," I apologize, smiling sheepishly. I lean in, my lips brushing against her ear. "Just thinking about all the things I'd love to lick off your naked body."

Her eyes widen, and her cheeks and ears redden. The girl can't hide a blush even if she tries.

It's cute and sexy as hell. I'll bet her chest is flushed too. I'd love to see that color all over her naked body.

Sadie clears her throat and squeezes my hand hard. Like she's trying to bring me back to reality.

Damn.

The fantasies were fun but fleeting.

"How long are we going to fake date?" Sadie asks. Her voice is soft and hardly above a whisper. "Just tonight, right?"

"Give me three dates."

"What?" Her eyes widen, and she's a little too loud, since Allie turns around and glances at the two of us.

"Everything okay?" Allie asks.

"Yes, Margherita's is just the next block," Sadie says.

"Margherita's?" I repeat. I let Sadie pick the restaurant, since I wasn't sure what her kid would eat.

Fuck.

The Italian Mafia owns Margherita's. I can't step foot in there without starting the next war. And now that I'm back working for the bratva, I must tread carefully.

"How about I take you both someplace a little fancier?"

"Margherita's is plenty fancy. Besides," her voice drops lower, "I don't know how you plan to pay for dinner, and I just lost my job."

"I'm working at the club, where I used to work at night. The pay is good, don't worry, it's my treat."

"Allie," I shout, and gesture for her to come back so we can discuss dinner.

She jogs toward us. "Yeah?"

"Margherita's is too Americanized for Italian food." I don't want to scare her and tell her that the Italian Mafia runs it. I mean, how would someone know that unless they're connected?

"I like it," Allie shrugs.

"There's a seafood restaurant across the street and a steak house the next block. Do either of those sound good?" I hope the kid wasn't planning on getting a pizza because there are no good pizza joints nearby.

"I love seafood." Allie's eyes light up.

I glance at Sadie, hoping she's onboard as well. "Sounds good to me."

At the next crosswalk, we head to the seafood restaurant, and while I didn't make reservations, I've done business with the owner in the past, and they seat us right away.

"No wait?" Sadie whispers into my ear. She raises an eyebrow. "Who are you?" she teases.

Allie doesn't seem to notice, and as we're escorted to our seats, she plops down at the table before I can pull her chair out for her. I pull Sadie's chair out, and she sits. I help push her back toward the table.

I sit at the table and glance over the menu, allowing a moment of quiet before the show begins. Up until now, it was the preshow, the appetizer.

It's game on.

When the waiter arrives at the table, he takes Allie's order first and then Sadie's. I'm grateful to be last because there are multiple items that look delicious.

It's been a while since I've eaten here. I finally settle on the Blackened Sea Bass topped with crab meat and Creole sauce. I haven't tried it yet, but everything I've eaten here is to die for.

The minute the waiter leaves, Allie is on me with questions. "How did you and Mom meet?" The girl knows how to put me on the spot. She'd be a great interrogator.

I glance at Sadie. We should have discussed the specifics before dinner and our fake date.

"At the park. Your mom was going for a jog, and I got hurt. She helped me," I say. Has Sadie told Allie anything about us?

"Is that why you have that scar?" She points at my forehead. It still looks fresh, but it's likely faded since the incident. I have older scars that she can't see, ones on my chest from being stabbed as a teenager when I first was indebted to the bratva.

The work I do is dangerous. So are the people I associate with, which is why I swore I would never involve anyone else. And here I am, having dinner with Sadie and Allie. No one will harm the girls while we're here. I don't have to watch my back or the kitchen constantly. They'd likely have poisoned our food if we'd eaten at the Italians'.

"It is," I say. The most straightforward lies are the ones fabricated around the truth. "What about you?" I ask, turning the questions onto her. "Do you have a boyfriend?"

Allie drapes her cloth napkin over her lap. "No."

"Girlfriend?" I ask.

"No, but that's very modern of you to ask. I like him already," Allie says. There's a huge smile on her face.

Is that all it takes? I'd have thought it would have been a lot harder.

"As long as we're asking the personal questions," Allie says. There's a glint in her eyes. I don't know what's coming, but I suspect I should be nervous. "You're the first guy Mom's brought home—ever. What are your intentions?"

"Allie!" Sadie scolds her daughter.

"I have to look out for you," Allie says, folding her arms across her chest. She's protective as hell.

I quirk a grin. "It's okay. I understand your concern," I say, trying to ease her daughter's mind. "I care about your mother very much." Again, not a lie. It's easy to admit that, considering she's such a good person. She helped me immensely. Do I not owe her the same back?

"But what are your intentions?" Allie asks, gesturing with her hands. "Are you going to marry her?"

"That's enough!" Sadie's cheeks burn, and her eyes are bright and wide. "I'm sorry, Dmitri. I don't know what's come over my daughter."

"No, it's fine," I say, trying to remain calm. "I understand where she's coming from. She wants to make sure that I'm not going to hurt the two of you. And I promise I will do everything to ensure that will never happen."

"Dmitri," Sadie's tone is a warning.

The charade has to end eventually. We're just doing this to keep Allie from suspecting what happened. The kid doesn't need to know that her mom was drunk, and I'm not much of a gentleman.

I didn't force her to have sex. I'm not a monster. But my desires always win.

"Dmitri and I are taking things slow," Sadie says. "We don't want to rush into anything."

"Except for bed," Allie quips.

Sadie's mouth drops, shocked by her daughter's remark. "When we get home—"

I take a sip of water and clear my throat, interrupting Sadie's threat. "That's enough, Allie. You need to show some respect to your mother."

The teenager rolls her eyes, not that I'd expect a thank you. "I don't think I like you very much anymore."

I shrug, not the least bit bothered. "That's fine. You don't have to like me. Most people don't. I'm used to it," I say a little too flippantly.

Sadie's brow is pinched. She wants to ask about my remark but thinks better of it. Her tongue darts out and swipes the top of her lip.

I reach for her hand, and she takes it, squeezing mine. It's more of a friendship handhold without our fingers interlocked together.

"Mom, he's lame. You should ditch him for the waiter. He's got dreamy eyes."

"He's a bit too young for my taste. I prefer my men aged, with some experience."

"Ewww." Allie's nose scrunches, and her eyes pinch closed. "That's disgusting."

"Then stop trying to pick out my dates for me. I'm perfectly content with Dmitri."

"Perfectly content?" I don't like the sound of that. She should be screaming on the rooftop how good the sex is and that she wants no man other than me. That no one else compares. I squeeze her hand with a grin. "That means there's room for improvement."

Sadie presses her lips together, her cheeks red. "Content is good. It means I'm happy."

Since picking her up, I've lost count of the number of times I've caught her blushing. Why is that?

"You two are gross," Allie quips. She reaches for her water glass and swirls it like a wine glass. "I'm glad Mom never invited me out on any of her dates before because you two are gross AF."

"Gross AF?" I ask.

"Gross as fuck," Allie answers.

"Allie!" Sadie scolds her daughter, but the teenager just shrugs.

"What? He asked, Mom. I wouldn't have said fuck if he didn't ask."

Sadie forces a smile as she stares into my gaze. "Are you sure you want to date someone with a teenager?"

That's the easiest out that she's given me, but I'm not about to take it. We haven't discussed how we'll break up from our fake relationship, but it's not about to be over her daughter. That's the worst idea ever.

"I'm not dating you because of your daughter," I say. That's an outright lie. The whole reason that we're on this fake date and in a fake relationship is because of Allie.

Although the date feels real to me. Just a little different than what I'm used to. I've never dated a woman with a kid before, let alone one who has a teenager.

Allie is aging me quickly.

Most of the time, the women I date, it's more a matter of picking them up at a bar for a dose of spicy foreplay and sex. There isn't wining and dining with my usual crowd. And they're never older than twenty-three or twenty-four. I tend to flock toward women who don't want a commitment. They prefer to be free, single, and looking for a night of fun.

It's a win-win if you ask me.

Sadie hasn't admitted to me that she wants anything more, and why would she? This isn't real.

Her feelings are an act. The blush on her cheeks is probably because she's nervous about lying to her daughter.

After dinner and dessert, I walk the girls back to Sadie's apartment. "You can't come inside," Allie says as we approach the building. "It's being fumigated."

It's a blatant lie. The girl cannot fib, which is probably good for Sadie's sake. "Is that so?" I ask. "Surely you shouldn't be going inside if it's fumigated. It isn't safe."

Allie glances at her mom for help.

"You're on your own for this one," Sadie says with a wicked grin.

The teen scrunches her nose, rolls her eyes, and stomps inside the apartment foyer.

"I'd offer you to come inside, but maybe it's not such a great idea," Sadie says.

I pull her against me. With one hand around her waist, the other pushes her hair back out of her face. "She's watching," I say, and glance in the foyer window.

"Oh," Sadie whispers. "Then I guess we should kiss."

It isn't the first time we've kissed, but it's the first time we're both completely sober. I lean in but pause, enough to make her finish the distance as I tease her. My fingers tangle in her hair, and her eyes are on my lips.

She sighs softly and dips her head toward me. It's like fireworks. The warmth she exudes flows through me and makes my heart pound in my chest.

I pull her close against me, tight, wanting to feel every inch of her body. We get lost together, her fingers at the nape of my neck, teasing along my collar.

I swear I hear her purr as my lips move to her neck. "We should—I can't let you inside. That's what started this mess."

She's right, and I hate that I have to listen and accept her terms. What I wouldn't give to bend her over and drive my cock inside her for the world to see.

I lean in, taking one last taste, nibbling on her bottom lip, tugging it between my teeth before letting go.

Another moan. Her panties are probably dripping wet.

My cock stirs, and I hate pulling away, but I have to before I embarrass both of us.

"Have a good evening, *Malishka*."

SEVEN

SADIE

My heart slams against my ribcage as I shut the apartment door. I lean back against the wood, letting it hold me up. My legs are like rubber from that kiss with Dmitri.

Why did I think kissing him out front on the porch would be a good idea?

Allie is on the sofa, the television on, ignoring me. It's for the best. I need a minute to cool off since a cold shower would be too obvious.

I head for the fridge, the cold air helping just a little as I reach for a bottle of wine. Dmitri hadn't ordered us alcohol during dinner. He hadn't even offered.

Was it because it wasn't a real date? Or maybe it had more to do with Allie being at dinner?

Allie has seen me drink a glass or two of wine. I haven't gotten drunk around my kid. I know better than to let her see me trashed after a night out with my friends. That's when I have her spend the night with a friend or over at the neighbor's so I can unwind.

Which only made things worse.

I slip out of my heels, leave my phone on the counter, and pour a glass of red. The taste is sweet and juicy. Delicious.

Tomorrow, I need to buckle down on finding a new job. I've spent the past few days applying and tidying up my resume, but I will need money to pay the bills soon.

I place my glass of wine on the dining room table and grab the laptop, bringing it with me to sit. I tap at the computer, open a web browser and glance at job openings. Allie is enthralled in whatever romance reality show is on.

There are a couple of listings for clerical work, a bar, and a strip club. I'll pass on the strip club, but I could work at a bar. I bartended years ago. Not one of my favorite jobs, but it paid the bills.

I jot down the information on a scrap of paper. The listing says to apply at the location, and they aren't taking online resumes.

How old-school is this bar?

"I'm going to run out for a bit," I say, shutting the computer and pouring the rest of the wine glass out. I don't want to be inebriated when I show up and ask for an application, but it's not like they're going to interview me.

"Sneaking out to be with your boyfriend?" Allie snickers.

"I don't have to sneak out. I'm an adult."

"Whatever. I'm watching my show." She waves me off, her gaze on the television.

It's Saturday night. The bar has to be crawling with guests. I type the address into my phone and grab a paper copy of my resume, slipping it into a leather folder. I'm still in my black dress, which is presentable enough for an application. It's not interviewee attire, but at least I'm not in jeans and a t-shirt. I grab a blazer to help with the ensemble.

"Okay, bye," I say. It's a relief that she's not asking any more questions because, at some point, I will have to tell her I changed jobs, which is fine once I find another gig.

I hurry out of the building and to the subway, taking the train across town. It's a couple of blocks and getting dark, but the roads are well lit. There's enough foot traffic at this hour that I don't feel isolated.

It's relatively safe.

I double-check my phone for the bar's address before glancing ahead and seeing it. I hurry inside, past the bouncer. He doesn't bother to check my ID. I'm not sure whether to be offended or flattered. The music is loud, pulsating through the club. There's a crowd at the bar, and I don't want to interrupt the bartender while he's busy.

I glance back at the bouncer. "Hey, I wanted to fill out an application. I saw your listing online that you're hiring."

He glances me over from head to toe and doesn't give so much as a hint of what's running through his mind. "We're busy." His accent is thick. Italian.

"I know. That's why I think I can help," I say. "I've bartended and waited tables. I've also worked at a hotel and handled customer issues. I'm a fast learner and quick on my feet. I'm just looking for an application."

He pulls a walkie-talkie from his belt loop. I hadn't even noticed there'd been one secured to his hip. "Boss, a girl is looking for a job here."

"Send her back to my office," an Italian voice answers through the walkie-talkie.

The bouncer points toward the back of the club. "Follow the hallway around back. It's that way."

I heed his directions and come to a frosted glass door that's slightly ajar. I give a firm knock, and it opens farther.

"Come in," an Italian male says. He gestures for me to join him in his office.

I step inside and close the door, the noise and boisterous music vanishing inside the room. "You have decent soundproofing in here," I say.

"Can't let myself get distracted." He offers a fake smile. It's all pleasantries. I don't think he cares for me, or maybe he doesn't care that I'm here.

"I don't mean to come by unannounced. I was hoping to get an application for an opening at your establishment. I noticed you have an opening for a bartender. I have five years of bartending experience."

"Is that your resume?" he asks.

I glance at his nameplate on the desk, Antonio Moretti. He has the darkest eyes I've ever seen, although it could be the dim lighting to blame.

"It is," I say, and open the leather folder, handing him the thick ivory paper with my details.

"Why do you want to work here?" Antonio asks.

"The way I see it, you need me. Your bartender is busy, and I'm sure he's not slow, but there's a line, which means either aggravated customers who will leave, or they order fewer drinks, because he can't keep up, and they go home."

His jaw is firm, and he places the resume on the desk, folding his arms across his chest. "I'll have to check your references."

"I would expect nothing less," I say.

"You'll have to work the rush shift every weekend. The customers tip well, but there go your Friday and Saturday nights."

"I won't miss them," I say. It'll be difficult not being with Allie in the evening, but I trust my daughter, and I'll be home late at night. She won't be entirely alone. I refrain from commenting on the fact that I have a daughter; it won't land me this job, and I need it so I can keep a roof over our heads and food on the table.

Sure, I have a few dollars in savings but not enough to live off indefinitely. New York City is expensive.

"You start tomorrow night," Antonio says. "Welcome to the family."

"Thank you." It's an odd choice of phrase, but I don't make anything of it. Perhaps the business is family-owned, or he likes treating his employees like family.

Antonio gives me the basic scoop on what time I need to arrive tomorrow, base pay, and the rules. He's not in the office often, and I'm to report up through another staff member. I thank him when I leave and walk back toward the subway.

It was dark when I left, but now the crowds have thinned on the streets.

I don't mind walking alone, but I keep an eye on my surroundings as I approach the subway. It's not overly crowded, but the trains run less often, and more people congregate by the platform as I wait for my train home.

A train pulls up at the station on the opposite side of the tracks. It's heading in the wrong direction for me to go home. Passengers disembark, and I swear I catch sight of Dmitri heading up the escalator.

Where's he going at this late hour?

I shouldn't be curious.

It doesn't matter.

I consider following him, but he'll think I'm stalking him, and I'm not sure he's wrong. Already, I'm arguing with myself over what happens if I'm caught.

My train pulls up.

I need to get in and head home. Get some sleep. And maybe steer clear of any more wine for the night.

————

The following day, I awaken to a text from Dmitri.

Had fun with you and Allie last night.

Sitting up in bed, I pull the covers up around myself. I start typing and erase my message, unsure what to say.

Me too. Should we talk about our breakup?

I hit send and hope that I haven't made a mistake. Should I have suggested we just do the breakup via text? I mean, it's not a real relationship anyhow. Except, I don't want to end things with him.

My phone immediately buzzes with a notification that he's calling.

"Good morning," I say.

That was quick.

"Morning, *Malishka*," Dmitri says. "How'd you sleep?"

A smile grazes my face. I shouldn't feel so damn giddy when talking to him. He's just a friend, one whom I slept with. It's no big deal. "I slept well. What about you?"

"The best night of sleep since being unconscious for what—six weeks?"

"That's not funny." He shouldn't be joking about his coma, but maybe it's how he's processing the trauma of what happened.

"Do you want to get breakfast this morning?" Dmitri asks.

I glance at the clock. It's just past eight. Allie will be asleep for at least another two hours. Breakfast would be just the two of us. "Yeah, that'd be nice."

"Great, it's a date."

I clear my throat at his remark. "Dmitri," I say, my tone holding a hint of warning.

"It's just an expression, relax. I'll swing by shortly."

I glance down at my pajamas. "I need to get dressed."

"Is twenty minutes enough time?"

Barely. The man doesn't know how long it takes a woman to look presentable. "I need to shower."

"You could wait for me, and we could shower together," Dmitri says.

My stomach fills with butterflies. "We could, but there's no way that Allie won't hear us." It'd be impossible to keep quiet with his hands on my body and my insides aching for him to fuck me.

A heavy sigh escapes my lips, and I bite down hard on my bottom lip when I realize he can hear me.

He chuckles under his breath. "How about I'll be there in forty-five minutes? It'll give you enough time to take a nice, hot shower."

I try not to whimper at the fantasies burning in my head of him pushing me up against the shower stall and fucking me from behind.

"Great. I'll see you in a bit." I don't comment on his hot shower remark. It could have been innocent, and he didn't mean anything sexual.

Who am I kidding?

He offered to come over and shower together.

Dmitri chuckles. "Think of me when you come, *Malishka*."

I moan involuntarily. The man is my absolute undoing.

"Did you just purr?" Dmitri asks.

I end the call and hurry for the shower, refusing to answer his question.

What the hell has he done to work me into such a frenzy? I inhale a deep breath and swear I can smell his masculine scent throughout my bedroom. It's intoxicating.

A sane person would wash the sheets.

I want to roll around in them and bathe in his fragrant aroma, making my insides pulse and shudder.

Fuck.

I should not care this much about a man I hardly know. A man who, by all accounts, I'm fake dating because I got caught with him over at the house while my daughter was away for the night. I feel like a teenager, hiding that I'm dating a boy from my parents.

Except I'm the adult, and Dmitri and I aren't dating.

When did my life get so fucked up?

I turn the shower on and wait for the hot water to warm up. How will I face Dmitri for breakfast in under an hour when my body is tingling with the thought of straddling his hips and riding him cowgirl?

What the hell has gotten into me? Why has he made me so damn horny?

I strip out of my clothes, and there's a prominent knock on the front door. I grab the white terry cloth robe hanging in my bathroom and slip it on. Padding out of my bedroom, I head for the front door and glance through the peephole.

I thought he was going to give me forty-five minutes. It's been what—five minutes?

I command Kona to sit while I yank open the door.

"Dmitri?"

His cheeks are red, and there's a primal look behind his darkened gaze.

His hands are on me, pulling me close and tight. His mouth descends hungrily on mine as though his life depended on it for survival.

"I haven't even stepped foot into the shower," I mutter between kisses.

"Good. It gives us plenty of time to get dirty first," he growls into my ear, nipping the lobe as his fingers pull me tighter. He walks me backward toward my bedroom and smacks the door shut with his foot.

"Lock it," I say. Allie is in the next room, and I don't want her to see anything.

He reaches behind him and hits the lock, giving us our privacy. He shucks out of his shirt and steps out of his shoes, following after me.

"I have the shower running." I head for the bathroom and untie the sashay around my waist, letting the soft white robe open, teasing him.

His eyes rake over my naked form, and he reaches for me, but I take a step backward toward the shower stall.

"Were you calling from the hallway?" I ask with a cheeky grin. I drag my fingers across his stomach and along the hem of his pants. I undo the zipper on his jeans, ridding him of his clothes.

Dmitri pulls me firmly against him. The robe falls to the floor at my feet. "I told you I wanted to have breakfast with you." His lips crash against mine, hungrily dueling for control. "I could eat you and be sated."

"Somehow, I doubt that." A giggle slips past as his fingers graze my hip and his touch is light. I'm ticklish, and while I don't think he's discovered the secret intentionally, it's obvious as I squirm out of his grasp.

"Ticklish," he says, taking note as he studies me with a wry grin.

"Shower, now." I slip out of his grasp and regain my composure. The shower is warm, and the bathroom is quite steamy. I step under the spray, and Dmitri follows me into the stall, standing behind me.

There isn't much cleaning or shampooing going on.

His hands are in my hair, tugging my mouth to his, keeping me under his control. I've never been dominated by anyone before, let alone a man I hardly know anything about. Dmitri is a mystery that needs solving.

He may have remembered who he is, but he's given me very little information. It's like he's hiding from me in plain sight.

My head dips back as his lips caress my neck and suck the sensitive skin. "Don't leave a hickey," I warn him.

"Why not?" He grins up at me. "Your daughter already thinks we're dating." He nips my neck as his hands caress my hips and tease across my stomach. He's slow, methodical, and isn't just diving in for the kill.

"You're such a tease," I mutter, and drag his lips back to mine.

He spins me around and shoves me against the cold tile wall, lifting me off my feet. I wrap my legs around him, my arms clinging to his neck. Our lips are fused with deep passionate kisses, each more intense than the previous.

"Fuck," he growls.

The water drowns out most of our sounds. At least, I hope it does as he guides his thick cock inside of me, stretching my insides. Moaning as he fills me, my fingers dig into his back, my nails marking his skin with each shallow thrust.

"You're killing me," I rasp, wanting him to go deeper. His motions are torture in the most delicious way possible.

"I doubt that." He kisses my neck and my lips. His eyes are heavy, and he stares into my soul, his breathing raspy. "Tell me what you want."

My lips part. Speaking exerts far more energy than I have available. "I want—you to—fuck me," I rasp, struggling to meet his stare. I want to shove my face into his neck and ride the orgasm. But he's not giving me every inch of his thick cock. "Deeper."

He tugs my bottom lip between his teeth, and the slight pain is mixed with pleasure as he drives his shaft inside my tight pussy.

My mouth parts, and I gasp as our bodies blur together as one.

Fuck.

Each thrust is more powerful, like a rising current, and I'm about to drown.

I gasp for breath. My insides clench onto his cock, the first of many spasms tingling through me like a jolt of electricity.

Dmitri slides out, leaving me to stand on wobbly legs.

"What?" I gasp, staring up, desperate for more. I was so close to the fucking edge, and he deprived me of my sweet release.

He's smiling, and his cock is rock hard.

"You're an asshole," I mutter.

His hand grabs my jaw, bringing my lips hard against his before he spins me around to face the wall, the cold tile at my cheek as he parts my legs, and his fingers graze my bottom hole. I gasp from the contact and anticipation. Is he teasing me, or will he drive his cock into my bottom?

I've never done that before. I'm not sure how I feel about it.

"Do you trust me?" Dmitri asks.

I nod.

"I need verbal confirmation."

"Yes," I whisper.

"Keep your hands on the wall." He presses my hands against the tile and then backs my hips toward him. I'm leaning forward, my butt sticking out, half-bent forward. I glance over my shoulder at him as he caresses my bottom and smacks my ass.

My cheeks clench, and I gasp from the contact.

"Did you like that, *Malishka*?"

"Yes," I gasp, surprised by my admission.

One hand caresses between my folds, discovering my wetness. "Do you want me to let you come?"

"Yes, please."

"Not yet," Dmitri says, and I swear he's smiling, but I can't see his face. My insides quake and shudder. My pussy throbs for release, and he's teasing me with his fingers, caressing my labia and my wetness but avoiding my aching clit.

My thighs clench, wanting him to hit that perfect spot.

He smacks my pussy. "Is that what you want?"

"Yes," I rasp, and my jaw hangs open, drinking in the air, my insides throbbing and pulsating. I'm so close, and he's not even fucking me.

"God, you're so fucking hot, Sadie. I want to drive my cock into your tight little hole."

"Which one?" I rasp.

He chuckles at my question. "That's a good girl." His finger wanders over my bottom hole, pressing lightly at the entrance, forcing me to squirm with anticipation.

"Is that what you want? Do you want me to touch you here?"

"Maybe?" I squeak.

"I need a yes or no, Sadie."

When he says my name, it makes me tinker on the edge. My head is in a fog, my body entirely his for the taking.

"Yes," I whisper, surprised by my admission.

His finger continues teasing my bottom hole, but he doesn't push past the entrance.

My hips squirm and rock as I feel the head of his cock teasing my pussy from behind. "Please," I pant. He's making me desperate. My hips thrust, wanting him, hoping that he'll let me reach release.

"I want you so bad," Dmitri rasps, and nibbles my ear. "But your bottom will have to wait. I want to fuck your tight pussy first."

I gasp, and his hand grazes my stomach and down into my curls as he thrusts his cock deeper inside me. He stretches me, pounding into my warmth. My insides spasm, growing near.

Each thrust is more powerful, and I tighten around his cock as fireworks explode inside me.

———

We should be talking about our inevitable breakup.

But all I can think about is bringing Dmitri home and fucking him again. He's a drug that I'm addicted to and all I think about. And I hate myself for it.

Sitting across from him at breakfast, my eyes rake over him.

"See something you like?" Dmitri asks. There's a smirk adorning his face, and the room feels several degrees hotter than a few seconds ago.

He's not talking about the plate of food he ordered in front of him.

I reach for my glass of orange juice, taking a swig for a much-needed distraction. "Were you hanging outside my apartment this morning when you called?" I ask.

"Something like that," he answers cryptically, and takes a bite of his bacon. "I need a favor."

"Yeah, sure," I say with a shrug, and place the half-empty glass on the table. I retrieve my fork and pick at my food. My stomach is filled with butterflies. What could he possibly need from me?

"A friend of mine is getting married, and I need a date for his wedding."

"And you want me to be that date?" I ask.

"I want you to be my fake girlfriend."

I laugh under my breath. The lines have already blurred, and he wants to continue this little charade between the two of us?

"What does that entail?" It's not like we haven't kissed or tangled in the sheets. And Dmitri isn't bad on the eyes. Pretending to be his girlfriend isn't the worst request.

"Two dinners and a wedding."

"What?" I squeak, my voice higher than I intend. "Three dates? I'm not that good of an actress." Maybe I could pull off one date or a wedding where his friends aren't paying that close attention to us, but on three separate occasions?

Is he trying to torture me?

"My friends want to meet you," Dmitri says.

"They can't meet me at the wedding?"

"There's also the rehearsal dinner the night before the big day. Come on. I'm helping you with Allie."

"We're supposed to be breaking up." Did he forget the plan?

"And we will after the wedding. We'll go our separate ways. No big deal." He takes a swig of his coffee. "What do you say?"

He pins me with his stare. "I helped you with Allie," he reminds me.

That was one night. This is three separate occasions. "Fine." I groan and snatch one of his sausage links from his plate. "If we're pretending to date, I can steal food off your plate."

A wicked smile crosses Dmitri's features. "You can have anything of mine you want, sausage included."

I snort at his remark, and I'm confident I'm blushing.

"Anything? I'm going to hold you to that," I quip.

EIGHT

DMITRI

"Really? You have a girlfriend?" Luka isn't convinced I'm seeing a girl, and we're serious.

Why should he be? It's not like he's ever seen me spend time with a girl outside a bar. And he's right. Sadie isn't like the other girls I've slept with. She's different.

For starters, what we have isn't real. The sex, on the other hand, that's dynamite.

"Her name is Sadie," I say as if that'll suddenly make him believe me.

"And you're bringing her to the wedding?" His eyes narrow, unconvinced. "Is she your sister or something?"

"She's my girlfriend," I reiterate. "The things we've done would be illegal if she were my sister."

Luka chuckles under his breath and folds his arms across his chest. "Fine, but I don't believe you until I meet her. This girl could be a figment of your imagination. You do have a nice scar," he says, gesturing to the mark on my forehead.

"How about dinner Monday night?" I suggest. Mikhail has made it abundantly clear that I'm to tout my fake girlfriend around before the wedding.

And the truth is that I don't mind taking Sadie out, wining and dining the girl. I'd prefer it not to be in the company of the bratva, but I can't undo that mistake. Mikhail knows about her and wants to use the two of us to preserve his self-image.

Typical Pakhan. Only worried about his reputation.

"Monday, we can do it," Luka says. "Although I should warn you, Hannah is in her wedding planning phase. Right now, that's all she seems to talk about."

"Are you warning me that she might put ideas into Sadie's head?"

It's good that we're not serious, and this relationship is fake.

"Yeah, I swear that's all Hannah discusses with Madisyn and Lucy."

"Your wedding is in less than a month. I'm sure that it'll ease up after the wedding. Are you two going anywhere for your honeymoon?"

It's good to be back, in the thick of things. I hadn't realized how much I'd missed out on the past few weeks.

"I rented one of those overwater bungalows in the Caribbean." Luka pulls out his phone and shows me the bookmarked page with pictures of the villa. "The individual hut features a private infinity pool and above-water hammock."

"And glass floors," I say, taking note of the interior photographs. The villa is stunning, and I'm sure it cost Luka quite a bit to secure the place for a few days. "How long are you staying?"

"We're traveling to Montego Bay for two weeks. I got a deal since it was last minute, but don't tell Hannah."

I smile and shake my head. "Don't worry. Does she know that you're taking her to Jamaica at least, or is that a surprise too?"

"Oh, she knows where we're going for the honeymoon but not the villa. I look forward to her thanking me repeatedly." The grin on Luka's face is smug. He probably imagines all the filthy things he'll do with Hannah when they're alone together and newly married.

"Hopefully she likes the ocean and knows how to swim."

The smile falls from Luka's face. "Don't be a dick."

I throw my arms up into the air. "I'm serious. If the girl fears water, you're taking her to stay in a hut in the middle of the ocean."

"It's not the middle of the—oh fuck. I should probably find out."

"Just get Madisyn to ask her."

Luka shakes his head and rubs his jaw. "That woman can't keep a secret."

"She hid the fact that she was an FBI agent from Mikhail." If Madisyn wants to keep a secret, she's entirely capable of keeping her mouth shut.

Luka disagrees with me. "Madisyn and Hannah are best friends. Just—no. I'm not telling Madisyn anything. What about your girl?"

"Sadie? What about her?" Where is he going with his question? My stomach flops as his eyes light up like he just came up with a master plan bound to backfire on me.

"During dinner together, convince Sadie to ask Hannah about the ocean, swimming, whatever will make sure that this honeymoon idea is gold."

"You want me to talk to Sadie about your little honeymoon secret?" I run a hand through my hair. Sadie and I hardly talk as it is outside of our time together. We're not an actual couple that dates, texts, chit chats.

We're more like friends with benefits—who also help one another out.

"Well, since you're offering," Luka says, "that'd be appreciated."

———

I haven't seen Sadie since breakfast together. I've texted her several times to follow up and make sure she's available Monday evening for dinner. We haven't spoken on the phone. When I've tried calling her, it goes straight to voicemail, and the same when she's called me.

It's like our timing is completely off.

Which would be fine, except that I need to coach Sadie on what to discuss with Hannah.

I swing by Sadie's apartment, bringing two bouquets with me.

Allie opens the door and glances me over from head to toe. Am I supposed to get the kid's approval? "Are those for me?" Allie's eyes light up.

I'm relieved I thought ahead to bring her a bouquet again, even though she's not coming out with us tonight. "These are for you," I say, handing her the mixed bouquet. The roses are still in my grasp, wanting to give them to Sadie.

As long as we're pretend dating for my benefit, we've agreed to continue the charade in front of Allie. Otherwise, it'll only pose more questions. We don't want our plan to backfire.

"Thank you," Allie says. Her eyes brighten as she takes the flowers from me and scurries off into the kitchen.

"I think you've won her approval, again," Sadie says as she rounds the corner. She's wearing a dark purple dress that hugs her curves and black stiletto heels. The shoes alone make me rock hard, imaging her in nothing but them.

I clear my throat and try to silence my cock. "These are for you," I say, handing her the flowers.

"They're beautiful, but you didn't have to—"

"I wanted to," I say.

Does she not realize how special she is? We don't have to be in a real relationship for me to appreciate her.

After she handles the bouquet and puts the flowers in water, we head down to my vehicle. I open the passenger door, letting her enter before hurrying to the driver's side.

"Thanks again for doing this," I say. I pull out into traffic, and Sadie fixes her skirt. Her fingers drum over her legs.

"It's no problem. Allie has plans to binge some new show tonight, so you've got me to yourself."

I wish I had Sadie entirely to myself. It'd be far more enjoyable than pretending for the two of us to be a couple.

"We're having dinner with Luka and Hannah," I say, catching her up on tonight's events. We haven't concocted the story of how we met or anything relating to our relationship. I'm not too concerned. Luka isn't likely to ask much, and if he's right about Hannah's mindset, she'll be focused on the upcoming wedding, which should make tonight a breeze. "Luka is one of the men I work with, and he helps run the club where I work." His responsibilities to the club have grown since losing Anton.

"What kind of club?" Sadie asks.

Her innocence is so serene and sweet. "It's a strip club," I say, and glance at her briefly before returning my attention to the road.

"Oh." I must have left that out when I had texted her that I got my old job back. I'm sure I've told her I was security at a club. I'm less of a bouncer, but I watch the front door to ensure that no one uninvited steps foot inside, like the Italian Mafia or Columbian Cartel.

We've had trouble with them before. The Italians destroyed our club months ago, and Mikhail doesn't want a repeat performance. My job is to make sure those who step foot inside are welcome guests.

"Club Sage," I say. "I'm sure that I've mentioned it before."

"Just that you work at a club," she says, and shifts in the front seat, glancing at me. "Do you ever get dances from the girls at the club?"

"No, that would be highly inappropriate. Besides, I'm not paying for entertainment." I pull up to a red light. Traffic is heavy. Rush hour never seems to end in New York City.

"What about for free?" Her voice is soft, tentative. "Do they ever give you a dance because they like you or want something from you?"

"I'm not interested in the girls at the club," I say, and pin her with my stare.

She inhales a sharp breath, and I glance back at the road as traffic begins to inch forward.

I swear I hear a hint of jealousy in her question. And it shouldn't matter because we're not a couple, and this isn't a real relationship. But I've never even fantasized about any of the girls at the club.

They're cute, but most are too young and barely legal. I'm not into that. I prefer a lady with a bit more experience and luscious curves. A real woman, one who knows what she wants and doesn't play games.

With my attention on the road, I reach out, interlocking our fingers together. "Is this okay?" I ask. It's not like we haven't held hands in front of Allie, but this is a little more intimate and less of friends holding hands.

"Yes," she says. Her voice squeaks, and she clears her throat.

"Luka won't believe we're an item if there's not some physical touching between us. I tend to be affectionate toward the women I date."

"So, you've brought other women to meet your friends?" I swear there's a hint of jealousy in her tone.

"No, but they've seen me with other women," I say. While I don't get involved with any of the dancers at the club, I've hooked up with a handful of women at a bar or in the club off-hours when I'm not working.

I glance briefly at her as we slowly drive past the restaurant. There's no valet and no parking lot. This isn't one of the restaurants that we own, or I'd have a place to park. I head for the nearest parking garage.

"There is one other thing that we haven't discussed."

"What's that?" she asks.

I follow the other cars up through the parking garage until I locate a space. "I need you to ask Hannah if she likes the beach."

"That's a weird question."

"I know, but I fucked up with Luka, and now he's second-guessing his honeymoon plans. Can you help me out?"

"Of course," Sadie says with a warm smile. She squeezes my hand before we head out of the SUV.

Together, we walk the handful of blocks to the Greek restaurant Luka picked out. "I hope this is okay," I say, opening the door for Sadie.

"I've never eaten here, but it smells delicious," she says as we enter the restaurant.

Luka is already seated at a table with Hannah. He nods, and Hannah waves with a huge grin on her face.

I slip my hand in Sadie's as we walk through the restaurant toward our table. I release my grasp, pulling her chair out for her to sit.

"Thanks," she says, offering me a sheepish grin.

"Wow," Hannah says, and smacks Luka's arm. "You ought to do that for me."

"I'm marrying you, doesn't that count?" Luka asks. He grins cheekily and reaches for Hannah's hand, giving it a prominent squeeze.

We do our quick introductions as we get situated at the table.

Sadie smiles warmly, glancing over the menu and ordering before directing her question at Hannah. "How's the wedding planning going?"

Luka groans and unlatches his hand from his fiancée's while he reaches for his water glass, taking a sip. "I'm going to need something stronger," he mutters playfully.

Hannah elbows him. "I swear you were more romantic before you proposed."

"You two are cute together," Sadie chimes, a warm smile on her face. The girl fits in perfectly, like she was cast for this role and waiting her entire life to play it. "How did you two meet?"

"That's a long story," Hannah says with a laugh.

I avert my stare, and Sadie reaches for my hand, intertwining our fingers. The girl doesn't miss a beat.

"So, have you two talked about kids?" Hannah asks, changing the subject.

"I have a daughter," Sadie says. "She just turned thirteen."

"Oh wow, a teenager or what I'd love to call a built-in-babysitter. Can I get her number?" Hannah asks.

Sadie chuckles. "She doesn't have a cell phone, but I can give you my number and coordinate."

Hannah whips out her phone, ready to take on the information.

I glance at Sadie. She doesn't have to do this. Won't it complicate matters after we break up? She smiles reassuringly at me, and the girls exchange phone numbers.

"So, who is watching Bay while you are on your honeymoon?" I ask.

"We discussed bringing in a nanny at the house and then having her look after Bay while we're gone. We also have very close friends who are around to make sure that she's cared for," Hannah says.

"We've talked about it, but nothing happened," Luka says. "We can't dump Bay off on a stranger. She needs time to get to know the new nanny."

"I know. That's why Madisyn has offered to help too."

"And I'm sure Allie would be happy to come over and play with Bay after school. Dmitri mentioned that you two are getting married Labor Day weekend."

"That's right," Hannah says. "And then we're going to Jamaica for our two-week honeymoon."

"That sounds splendid," Sadie says. "I'll bet you're a beach girl. Sand. Sun. Surf?"

"I love swimming, but I've never gone surfing. Can we do that while we're in Jamaica?"

"We'll see," Luka says with a laugh and a wide grin. It's like the tension just seeped right out of him.

"What about the two of you?" Hannah asks. "Luka didn't tell me how the two of you met."

I glance at Sadie and answer before she can concoct a story. "Sadie went off the trails and got lost in the woods on a run. She stumbled onto me after I'd been shot." The story is close to the truth, but I don't want Luka or anyone else within the bratva suspecting that she might have witnessed anything.

"That could have been dangerous, getting lost in the forest," Hannah says. "See, that's why I don't run."

"I don't know. You chase after Bay a lot," Luka says.

They stare into each other's eyes, momentarily forgetting Sadie and I are at the same table. "Get a room," I mutter under my breath.

Sadie chuckles at my remark. "You don't feel that way about me?" she teases.

"Oh, I do, *Malishka*," I whisper, and my fingers travel below the table, resting on her knee.

I swear I hear the woman purr, and my cock twitches at the sound she makes.

"The things you do to me," I growl at her.

Sadie clears her throat and, while staring at me, nods toward the couple we're dining with as if they care about our little intimate moment.

Luka is staring at me, a wide grin on his face. "And you were saying?"

He's teasing me. It turns out he heard my comment about the two of them needing to get a room. I'd gladly get a hotel room with Sadie to worship her body and have the entire night to drive her wild and bury my cock inside her. But we can't leave her daughter home alone all night.

No one told me that dating a woman with a child would make things hard.

I shift uncomfortably on the chair. I need to turn the conversation onto anything that puts my dick back to sleep, at least for a little while. Although the deep purple dress that Sadie is wearing and the dip in cleavage doesn't exactly help.

She looks positively stunning and radiant.

I'm relieved when the waitress brings our dinners to the table.

"Everything looks delicious," Sadie says.

We dig into our meals, the conversation taking a momentary backseat while we eat.

"Does anyone want dessert?" I ask, pinning Sadie with my stare. I've eaten too much as it is, but I want any excuse to spend a few more minutes together on our fake date, which feels real.

"I'll split dessert with you," she says, her voice low and raspy.

My cock twitches in my trousers. I want to loosen my tie. The room is stifling. Did someone turn on the heat?

"Sadie, what do you do for a living?" Hannah asks.

The waitress clears the dishes from our table and brings two dessert menus for us to glance over.

"I'm bartending."

"You didn't tell me you found a new job," I say.

She forces a smile and is quick to correct me. "Yeah, I just started the other day."

"What's the place? We'll stop by for drinks sometime," Luka says.

I reach for my glass of water, my mouth dry. I'd love to stop by wherever she's working and tease the hell out of her. Flirt. Seduce.

"Moretti's," she says.

I choke on my water and place the glass hard on the table. Is she bartending at Antonio Moretti's bar? He runs the Italian Mafia! "You're not working for *him*." My tone drips with disgust.

"What? Why not?"

I can't even look at Luka or Hannah. However, I feel their heated stares piercing through me. I nod for

Sadie to accompany me, away from the table with our friends.

Her brow tightens, and she places her cloth napkin on the table as she stands. She accompanies me to the back of the restaurant in the hallway, just outside the bathroom.

"You can't work for Antonio Moretti."

"Do you know him?" Sadie asks. The girl has no idea how deep she's gotten in with the mafia.

"He runs the fucking Italian Mafia," I seethe. I run a hand through my hair. My heart is pounding against my ribcage. Anger pulsates through me. "How long?"

"What?" she frowns, unsure of my question.

"How long have you been working for him?"

"Just a few days. I needed a job and saw that the bar was hiring, and they were busy. The pay is decent, and the tips cover all my expenses and then some."

As if that will make me suddenly appreciate Moretti.

"No," I state.

"No, what?" Sadie asks. She folds her arms across her chest.

"You're not working for the Moretti family. He'll own you."

Sadie rolls her eyes. She doesn't get the gravity of the situation. "I already work for him, Dmitri. It's no big deal. Whatever you think he's doing, the business he runs where I work is clean. It's legitimate and safe. I'm fine. You need to chill out."

She turns to head back, presumably to the table. I grab her by the waist, turning her to face me. "We're not done here."

"Well, I am. Stop manhandling me," Sadie says, and shrugs out of my grasp.

She hurries back to the table, opens her purse, drops a few dollars on the table for her meal, and bolts out the front door.

"Fuck!"

NINE

SADIE

Who the hell does he think he is, telling me what I can and can't do?

Dmitri doesn't control me.

He doesn't get a say in where I work.

Hell, we're not even really dating! I'm fuming. My insides are boiling, and after I drop enough cash on the table to pay for my dinner, I hightail it out of the restaurant.

Antonio Moretti, the Italian Mafia? I don't believe it.

Yes, he's Italian, but just because he's of Italian descent, it doesn't automatically mean that he works for the mafia.

I've worked a handful of nights at the bar. I've seen nothing to prove Dmitri's story or anything shady.

Antonio is hardly around the bar. I met him on the day of my interview; that was the last time I saw him.

But that doesn't mean anything.

He's probably busy with other projects or handles other business matters during non-peak hours. He could run a second bar or a club.

Dmitri needs to get out of my head. I walk back in the direction of my apartment. It's too far to walk the entire way, but I'm steaming and need a way to unleash my boundless energy.

I've already walked several blocks when a black SUV pulls up alongside me. The back window rolls down.

Antonio Moretti sits behind the driver's seat while he has someone chauffeuring him around. He glances me over. "It's late, Sadie. Let me give you a ride."

I bite down on my tongue. There's no sign of Dmitri, not that it matters. He made his position clear, and I made mine just as crystal.

"Can you drop me off at my apartment?" I ask, stepping toward the SUV.

"Of course, just give the driver your address," Antonio says.

Dmitri is out of his mind.

There's no way this man is with the Italian Mafia.

Perhaps it's another Antonio Moretti, or Dmitri is just completely delusional. I open the back door, provide my address to the driver, and slip into the vehicle beside Antonio.

"I must say, I'm surprised to find you walking alone at this hour and quite far from your home, given the subway is in the opposite direction."

Antonio is observant. I'll give him that much.

"Bad date," I say, not wanting to elaborate further.

He chuckles and nods knowingly. "I remember those days before I married my *Tesorina* and settled down," he says.

I glance at his hand, noticing the wedding band.

If what Dmitri said were true and Antonio was the head of the Italian Mafia, what woman would marry him? He'd be a monster by Dmitri's definition.

I can't ask him if he works for the mafia. Even if he does, he's not going to out himself. Men like that are secretive because of their shady business dealings.

"What brings you down here?" I ask, pretending to make small talk. Every so often, I glance out the window to make sure that we're heading in the correct direction of my apartment.

I'm being paranoid. I blame Dmitri for my ridiculous concerns.

"I just dropped my daughter, Sophia, off at a sleepover."

If it weren't summer, I'd be wondering what type of parent drops their kid off on a Monday night for a sleepover, but Allie is out of school for a few more weeks, and I'm sure Sophia is as well.

"How old is Sophia?" I ask.

"She just turned five. The twins are growing up so fast," Antonio says.

"Twins?" I laugh. "I can't imagine having two of them at that age. I have my daughter, she's thirteen, and I swear that's all I can handle. One teenager at a time."

"I have a lot of help from my wife, Aleksandra."

"That's wonderful," I say. The way he speaks, it's clear that he admires Aleksandra. I can't imagine a man like that being the monster that Dmitri believes him to be.

We round the corner as we get closer to my apartment. "I hate to ask this," Antonio says. "But would you mind if I used your bathroom? I swear I'll only be a minute."

I open my mouth. Something tells me I should say no, but I can't find any logical reason to turn him down.

He's not the least bit forceful or brutal.

Antonio seems harmless. "Yes, of course. You'll just have to excuse the mess. I'm sure my daughter Allie has every snack out on the coffee table and kitchen. She's bingeing her new favorite reality show."

The driver pulls up out front of the building. He leaves the vehicle running, steps out and around, and opens the back door for me. I climb out first onto the sidewalk and wait for Antonio to follow.

"What show is that?" Antonio asks.

"Gosh. Aren't there so many to keep track of? Love Villa." I retrieve the keys from my purse and unlock the main entrance. We head to the elevator, and I push the button for the sixth floor.

"Aleksandra loves that show," Antonio says. "Although she has trouble bingeing it because of the twins. We've agreed to monitor what they watch."

"That's smart, especially when they're so young." I head out of the elevator once we reach the sixth floor, and he follows close behind. Unlocking the apartment, I let him inside.

"You're home early—" Allie says, and glances behind me with a frown on her face. She doesn't recognize Antonio, and why would she? She's too young to go to a bar, and while I finally told her I changed jobs, I didn't elaborate on the specifics.

I lead Antonio to the bathroom and flip on the light. "Here you go," I say.

He steps into the bathroom and closes the door behind himself.

"Who is he?" Allie asks, keeping her voice down. "Where's your boyfriend?"

"Long story," I say, and glance from Allie back to the bathroom. The fan is running, so I can't hear anything inside the small space. Not that I want to listen to him use the facilities, but my stomach is a bundle of knots after what Dmitri said.

Why did he have to get into my head?

"You owe me details," Allie says. "If I brought a strange man home, you'd want an explanation."

She's right, but I'm an adult. I do owe her the truth, at least partially.

The bathroom door opens, and Antonio reemerges. "Thank you," he says, offering a smile. I can't tell if it's forced or genuine. I don't know him well enough to read him, but he's given me no reason to distrust him.

Dmitri is paranoid.

"I'll see you at work tomorrow," Antonio says as I accompany him to the front door.

"Thanks again for the lift home." I walk him to the door and lock it behind him once he's gone.

Allie pauses her show and turns to face me, awaiting an explanation. "What happened on your date? Why'd mystery man from work take you home?"

"You heard that?" I'll have to be more careful around here if I don't want Allie overhearing something.

"Come on, Mom. You'd make me explain."

"Things went a little south on my date with Dmitri." I don't want to tell Allie why or she'll be worried about me when I see Antonio at work tomorrow night.

"South? As in the two of you broke up?"

"I don't know," I say. I slip out of my heels and sink into the couch beside my daughter. "It's complicated."

There's no point in telling her the breakup was inevitable since we weren't dating.

What is he going to expect from me? Will he still want me to attend his friend's wedding? It seems pointless since that friend saw our fight.

I tip my head back on the sofa and shut my eyes. "I hate men."

"Don't say that. Your work friend seems nice," Allie says.

I glance at her, and she's grinning widely.

"He's married." I don't mention that he has two kids. The fact that he's married is enough to stop me from showing interest in him.

"So, what happened with the boyfriend?" Allie asks.

The girl is persistent.

"Don't you have your show to watch?" I gesture at the television.

"No way, this is much more interesting. Real-life drama is a lot more intense." She wiggles her eyebrows. "Dish it."

I can't tell my thirteen-year-old daughter that my fake boyfriend insists that I'm working for a mafia boss. It sounds crazy in my head, and saying it out loud will only make it real.

"He's crazy," I say. "Dmitri has to be crazy." It's the only explanation I'll accept, because if he's right, I've already shown Antonio where I live, and he's briefly met my daughter. In my anger at Dmitri, I wasn't thinking clearly about my family.

My phone buzzes.

It's Dmitri.

"Are you going to answer it?" Allie asks. She peers at my phone, grinning even wider, like she's happy to see I'm suffering. I know that's not the case, but it sure as hell feels that way.

I groan and head out of the living room. I need privacy if I'm going to talk to him. I shuffle into my bedroom and shut the door. It takes me a second to regain my composure before I click to accept his call.

"What do you want, Dmitri?" I ask.

If he's calling to apologize, I'm not ready to hear it.

"Where the hell are you? It's late, and I've circled the neighborhood a dozen times looking for you."

"I'm home."

"Home? How did you get home?" He pauses for a beat. "You didn't take the subway. Hannah went in that direction and caught the train. You took a cab," he says, answering his question of how I got home.

"No, someone gave me a ride."

I'm not about to lie to him.

"You got into a car with a stranger?"

"He wasn't a stranger," I say. "Besides, you made it clear that you think you can put a leash on me and tell me who I can and can't work for. Well, you're wrong. This fake relationship is officially over."

I end the call, refusing to fight any more with Dmitri. We're not dating. We're not a couple. It's over.

I turn off my phone, not wanting to receive any more calls or texts for the night. I leave it on my bedside table to remove any further temptation before returning to the living room with Allie.

"Did he apologize?" Allie asks, watching me as I stroll across the room and sit beside her.

"No, but I didn't give him time to, either. It's over."

"I thought you really liked him?" Allie's brow is furrowed as she stares at me.

Is she waiting for me to cry?

We haven't been together that long. Hell, we haven't even really been anything more than friends with benefits. Yes, I'll miss the sex, but it's nothing that I can't satisfy with a new vibrator. Dmitri is a million times better than any vibrator I've ever owned, but it's not worth the headache.

What we had wasn't even real.

"Turn your show back on," I say, pulling my legs up on the sofa. I'm grieving inside, aching at the sudden loss of what?

He wasn't mine.

I need a distraction, and maybe Allie's show can make me forget Dmitri, even for a few hours.

I doze off on the couch.

The front door buzzer for the apartment rings, startling me from slumber.

"Don't get that," I mutter, rubbing my eyes.

Allie pauses her show.

"What time is it?" I ask. How long have I been asleep?

"Almost midnight." She knows she's supposed to be in bed already but got away with an extra late night because I fell asleep on the couch.

The buzzer sounds again.

I groan and stand, heading toward the door. I hit the button to communicate. "What?" I'm grumpy, and he's trying my patience.

I assume it's Dmitri. Who else would stop by the apartment at midnight on a Monday night?

"Can we talk?" Dmitri asks. His voice is calm, far more so than I would have anticipated.

"Call my phone."

"It goes straight to voicemail. Your phone is off."

"Yeah, I know. I didn't want to talk to you." Can't the man take a hint?

"I want to explain. Please, Sadie, give me five minutes. I'll leave after that, and you never have to see me again."

Allie is watching from the sofa. She's turned the television off because it's late and she's been caught, but she hasn't gone to bed.

"Five minutes." I press the button, allowing him inside the building.

"You're letting him in? I thought you hated him," Allie says.

"Bedtime." I point toward her bedroom.

Allie groans and drops the remote control on the sofa. "Fine. You're no fun when you're grumpy." She fusses the entire way to her bedroom, and I expect to hear the door slam shut, but it doesn't.

The kid is trying to eavesdrop.

Wonderful.

Privacy is a luxury that I don't have. And if I talk with Dmitri in the hallway outside my apartment, my neighbors will overhear everything.

And I don't want to lead him on by suggesting we talk in the bedroom.

There's a soft rap at the door, and I unlock it, letting Dmitri inside. "What?" I ask, folding my arms across my chest. I'm tired and not in the mood to deal with his possessiveness.

He stalks toward me, his brow pinched. "I was worried about you tonight."

"I'm fine." I take a step back, keeping ample space between us. I'm good with distance, putting a wall up around my heart. I've had years of practice.

"If it's over, that's fine, I can accept that, but I won't accept you are working for *him*."

"Are you jealous? Because I can't understand why else you would care who I work for."

"Antonio is a monster. He's responsible for dozens of crimes. He's not just a low-level thug, Sadie. The man is conniving and will take you down with him."

I sit on the chair opposite the sofa, where there's only one seat, forcing Dmitri to stand or sit across from me, keeping distance between us.

"I don't plan on doing anything illegal," I say. "Assuming what you're saying is true."

"It is." He steps closer. "I can assure you that it's one hundred percent the truth. He's not a good man."

I laugh under my breath. "Dammit, Dmitri. I'm not dating him. It's just a job. Why do you care so much who I work for?"

He inhales a sharp breath but doesn't answer right away. "He's dangerous, and I hate to see you get mixed up in his dirty work. He will take you down, blame you for his crimes."

"I'm a bartender, that's it," I say, emphasizing that I'm not involved in anything illegal. "There's a bouncer at the door checking IDs. I don't run the books or numbers. I'm not involved in dealing drugs, weapons, or whatever else you think he's smuggling and dealing."

He steps closer, my knees knocking against his legs. "I don't want to see you get hurt, or worse, him come after your family. Does he know that you have a daughter?"

"You're overreacting." I hope he's wrong, that Antonio isn't more than a family man, and Dmitri has him mixed up with someone else.

"I wish I were."

"Is that all?" I ask, waiting for him to drop another bombshell on me tonight.

"Dinner tonight was a bit of a disaster. Luka and Hannah are asking what happened. I need you to finish what we agreed on. Two more dates."

TEN

DMITRI

What a fucking disaster.

When Sadie announced her new job at Moretti's Bar, she may as well have shouted from the rooftop that she works for the Italian Mafia.

Talk about fucking me over.

If she wanted to get out of the date, all she had to do was say as much.

But the Italian Mafia?

They're our biggest enemy.

Not that she knows I work for the Russian Bratva. I've done well to keep my secret. After stopping by her apartment and discovering the girl is more bullheaded than I am, there's only one choice left.

Put a guard outside her building and have her under constant surveillance. It's not solely my orders. Mikhail demands the tail as well. He wants to reassure himself that she's not using me and reporting whatever secrets she thinks she knows to the Italians.

But I haven't told her anything.

Even so, I'm happy she has a guard watching her home. I feel better knowing that she's safe and Allie will be unharmed.

I keep a low profile with Sadie. It isn't particularly hard considering I have work five nights and the other two, I'm digging around for information on Anton's whereabouts.

A man like Anton doesn't just disappear.

And any connections he has are the same as Mikhail and the bratva. To vanish without a trace with Savannah is unheard of but not impossible.

He had help.

But from who?

Questions are ruminating in my head, making me toss and turn at night. If it's not my thoughts on Sadie keeping me awake, it's the fact that I was left for dead, and Nikita was driven to the hospital.

Something is off.

I can't use the bratva's resources without Mikhail being notified. During the afternoon, I head to a local internet café and use their resources to hire a private investigator. I give him as much information on Anton and Savannah as I can, using a burner cell phone to communicate with him.

I don't want anything traceable or tracked back to me.

I'm unsure what to do when we find Anton, but I need answers.

Exhausted, I rub the sleep from my eyes and force myself awake with a double espresso. I sip the scalding coffee and head out of the café. Rounding the corner, I nearly knock Sadie over.

"Are you following me?"

"No, I was working," I say.

She glances around. "Your club isn't around here."

I stare into her piercing gaze, sipping my espresso. "How would you know that?" I'm sure I've told her that I work at Club Sage, but I never divulged the location. It's doubtful she knew it without looking it up.

She doesn't answer my question. "It's two in the afternoon. What are you really up to?" She glances me over from head to toe and notices my coffee container. "An internet café?" Her brow is pinched.

"I'm just doing a little research."

"And you don't have a computer at home? I thought you were Bearded Bad Boy," she says, and I inhale a sharp breath.

"I am," I say, confirming her suspicions. Not that she has any idea I use the game console to help traffic guns, drugs, weapons—whatever Mikhail needs me to do. Conversations are untraceable. It's the perfect platform without rousing suspicion. "My laptop is getting fixed at the shop, so I'm stuck using this place until the repair is complete."

She nods, seemingly satisfied with my explanation.

While it's the afternoon, the streets are relatively crowded, and people are bustling through the city. I catch sight of Ivan watching from across the street. Sadie hasn't noticed him, and I shift slightly so that her back is to him, and she won't catch sight of him watching us.

"How is Allie?" I ask, changing the conversation.

"She likes you. Thinks you're a dick for not apologizing and sending me dozens of bouquets, chocolates, the works."

I can't tell if she's teasing. "I'll make a mental note."

"Are you... okay?" she asks before rolling her lips together. Does she want to ask me something else?

"Why wouldn't I be? It was just a fake relationship." I force a laugh.

"Not that," she says, and steps closer. She takes my hand, the one not holding my coffee, and squeezes it. "You were shot, Dmitri. I can't help but worry who did that to you and if they're coming back to finish the job." Her brow is knitted, and she's biting her bottom lip.

"You don't have to worry about me. I can take care of myself."

"Can you? Because I found you in the forest, shot, and you would have bled to death if I didn't call for help." There's concern laced in her tone. She squeezes my hand. She's worried about me. I don't know why she cares.

"You don't know that," I say. "I could have crawled to the nearest path and gotten someone's attention."

"You weren't budging when I ran over to you."

I'll have to take her word for it because I don't remember anything after we drove into the forest. The rest is a blur—a mental block.

"I don't remember," I say, staring into her concerned gaze. "But I'm fine. It was all a misunderstanding."

"Was it?" Sadie asks. "Because you know a lot about the Italians." She keeps her voice low, leaning into me to ensure no one can overhear us. But it's loud outside, and with traffic and dozens of pedestrians breezing by, I can barely hear her, and I'm right next to her.

"What are you saying?" I ask.

"Did the mafia shoot you?" Sadie asks. Her eyes are filled with concern.

It would be easy to lie to her and blame it on Antonio and his men. Perhaps she'd listen to me, leave that stupid bar, and come work for us.

I grimace at the idea of her working at Club Sage, even as a bartender. I don't want Nikita or Mikhail getting any ideas to put her on stage. I'd kill any man who looked at her like I do.

Shit.

What the hell has gotten into me?

Sweat licks my forehead, and I shuffle my feet, pulling Sadie away from the sidewalk and against the brick building wall.

Her hand rests on my hip as I pull her into the shade. Her touch is possessive.

Is it on purpose?

I can't fight the urge to kiss her any longer. I shove her up against the brick building, and my lips crash on her. I want to fuck her for the world to see.

But I settle for tasting her lips. My fingers caress her hair, deepening the kiss.

She moans, the sounds doing wild things to me, making me want to take her outside and show everyone she's mine.

Eventually, I break the kiss, resting my forehead against hers.

"I don't remember who shot me," I say. It's not a lie, but I remember who was in the vehicle that day: Nikita, Anton, and Savannah. One of them has to be responsible.

It takes her a moment to regain her composure. She looks at me curiously, like she can't remember the question.

I like that I've gotten inside her head.

Good. I like having that power over her—the ability to make her speechless.

She licks her lips where my tongue was moments earlier. Sadie exhales a nervous breath, staring up at me. "Please don't lie to me, Dmitri. Are you with the Italian Mafia?"

I want to laugh at her question. The absurdity of it is mind-boggling. Does she not realize that the Italians and Russians have two distinct organizations in the city?

She shouldn't know.

She can remain innocent of the darkness that surrounds us. The girl has no idea the depth of what she's stepped into.

Sadie is lucky that she isn't drowning.

"I'm Russian," I say. That's all she gets.

I won't lie to her. But telling her without her outright asking is absurd. She doesn't need to know I'm bratva. It certainly won't save her.

If she slips, it could get us both killed.

I'm not afraid of death, but I don't want to see Sadie or her daughter get hurt. They deserve better.

Her eyes narrow like she's trying to make sense of what I've told her. I wrap my arm around her shoulder and steer her away from the brick building and keep her close to me. "Can we move on from our fight?" I ask.

I want her to come to Nikita's wedding and be my date. I'd like her to attend the rehearsal dinner, and even though we're not a real couple, I enjoy her company and companionship.

"I think we did," Sadie says, glancing at me as we walk alongside one another. "As long as you can accept where I work."

I've got eyes on her all the time.

I'll be the first to know if anyone messes with her.

"I can do that," I say. With time, she'll quit. I know that without a doubt. Antonio will reveal his true colors, and when he does, she'll come running to me.

I just hope it doesn't frighten her, or worse.

But I can't lock her in a gilded cage. She isn't mine to protect. No matter how much I want to keep her safe, she's a grown woman intent on making her own choices.

No matter how foolish they may seem. And to give her proof that Antonio is with the Italian Mafia would only reveal my secrets and who I work for, the Russian Bratva.

"How is Allie?" I ask, glancing at Sadie as I walk beside her, keeping her close to me. If it were up to me, I'd never let her go.

"Good. She hates that she has to return to school in a few weeks, but other than that, she's a ray of sunshine."

There's definite sarcasm in her tone. "Is she getting under your skin being home all summer?" I ask.

She doesn't quite answer my question. "Allie has been asking about you nonstop. Wanting to know why I'm mad at you, why you haven't sent me presents to make up for your mistake, like in the movies..." her voice trails off.

Was I supposed to send her a present? That's news to me. The girl is working for the enemy. That doesn't exactly scream chocolate-covered strawberries.

"Well, tell her we've worked it out like adults."

"I'll be sure to mention that the next time she asks." She nudges against me.

Her lips are red and swollen from our heated kisses.

"Do you want to come over tonight?" she asks.

"I do, but I have to work tonight."

"Shit, so do I." She laughs and smacks her forehead, tipping her head back. "Sometimes I'm such an idiot."

"Never," I say, squeezing her hand as I interlock our fingers together. "Next day off?"

"Wednesday."

"Me too," I say.

"Sounds like a date."

———

I didn't have Wednesday off, but I convinced Nikita to let me switch the schedule because I need to fix this thing with Sadie.

He still thinks we're a real couple, fighting it out after discovering where she works.

But Nikita is ultimately supportive of the entire situation since Sadie is unaware that we're bratva.

I don't care. The fact is that I like her a lot. She ought to be off-limits, but I found her before the Italians. Doesn't that make her *mine?*

Except our relationship is entirely fake, minus the sex. That's real.

Talk about fucking complicated.

Instead of bringing flowers like the last two times I've taken her out, I'm carrying a box of chocolate-covered cherries and strawberries tonight. A mix that I hope she'll let me feed to her, in bed, naked.

Ivan is standing guard outside the building, ensuring no familiar Italian faces appear. "You can go home," I say. "I'll keep an eye on her tonight."

Ivan grins and smacks my arm before retreating down to his vehicle.

I press the buzzer, letting her know I've arrived for our evening together. It's not technically a date since we're not a couple. It's just enjoying each other's company.

More importantly, the opportunity to rip her clothes off and enjoy every inch of her body.

The front door opens, and I hurry into the elevator, pressing the button for the sixth floor. The elevator is stuffy, and I'm even wearing my suit coat and tie.

I'm dressed much more casually for tonight. After all, aren't we going to rip each other's clothes off anyhow?

Dark-washed blue jeans and a white shirt with a collar make up my ensemble. I loosen a button on the dress shirt.

Did someone turn the heat on in the building? It's summer, for fuck's sake. It's air conditioning season.

Hopefully, the chocolate treats don't melt on my way upstairs. I suppose if they do, I'll have to dribble the dessert over Sadie's naked torso and lick the sweets right off her body.

The elevator doors open at a snail's pace, and I slip out before the doors are fully open. I hurry down the hallway and give a prominent knock on the door.

There are footsteps, and then Allie pulls the door open, glancing me up and down. "No flowers?" She folds her arms across her chest, unimpressed.

"I brought dessert," I say, revealing the box in my right hand.

Allie's eyes light up. "Great. Because you'll be starving after you see what Mom made."

I breathe a sigh of relief when she lets me inside the apartment. I shut the door behind myself and slip out of my dress shoes, noticing everyone else's shoes by the front entrance.

"It smells good in here," I say.

Sadie is laboring in the kitchen, standing over the stove, preparing dinner.

"You have to say that," Allie chimes, stepping into the kitchen. "He brought you a present."

I reveal the box of chocolates to Sadie, placing it on the empty counter. "Can I give you a hand?" I offer.

"Do you mind helping Allie set the table for dinner?"

"Happy to help," I say.

Allie barely helps, deciding instead to delegate by showing me where everything is located. I imagine that Sadie has her hands full with the girl, and I can't even fathom what it'll be like when Allie is driving and dating.

Dinner consists of blackened fish on the iron skillet, asparagus, and a garden salad. There's also a fruit bowl on the table with fresh peaches that haven't been sliced. They look delicious along with everything else.

It turns out Sadie is a decent cook, although Allie picks at her plate, pushing the food around more than eating it.

"You don't like fish?" I ask, trying to engage Allie. I can't tell if she's not hungry or if something else is bothering her.

"It isn't that," Allie says, dropping her fork. It clanks against the plate with a shrilling sound. "Mom won't let me visit my cousin, Olivia."

"They just moved to Nova Scotia," Sadie says. "Have you ever been there?"

"Can't say that I have." I finish the last of the food on my dinner plate. The meal was terrific, and Sadie's cooking surprised me, especially given Allie's comment when I arrived for dinner.

"It's gorgeous," Allie says. Her eyes brighten with every word she speaks. "Olivia's been sending me pictures. I really want to go, and I have another week until I have to be back for school."

"Do you know how expensive it is to fly last minute?" Sadie asks, staring at her daughter. "You have no concept of money, Allie."

"I know you have money saved and can totally afford to send me to visit Olivia. You just got a new job. I'll bet it pays more than you were making at the hotel. Come on, please." Allie's bottom lip jets out, pouting.

"We're not having this conversation at the dinner table with our guest."

"He's your boyfriend," Allie says, and shrugs like it's no big deal.

"I could find out if the private jet is available, and we could take a family trip up there together."

Allie's eyes widen, and her mouth hangs agape. "You have a private jet?"

"Dmitri," Sadie warns, "that's too much."

"I can't make any promises, but if it's available, I can request the flight and time off from work."

Sadie sighs and pinches the bridge of her nose. "I'm not sure that I can get time off. I just started my new job, Allie."

"Dmitri could take me." Allie glances with wide eyes from me to her mother.

"I don't think that's what Dmitri wants to do on his vacation," Sadie says.

She's right. Spending time with the two of them would be fine, but shuttling Allie to Canada doesn't sound exciting. But at least she's not suggesting that we go in the middle of winter.

"Ask your boss for time off," Allie says. "Do the flirty thing."

"The flirty thing?" I ask, pinning Sadie with my stare. What the hell is she doing around Antonio? The man is married and one of the most vicious and ruthless men I know.

Sadie's cheeks redden as she plays with her hair, twirling a strand around her finger as she stares into my gaze. There's more to it, but she's not showing all her secrets to her thirteen-year-old daughter.

"I don't flirt with just anyone," she says, pinning me with her stare.

My mouth is dry, and I reach for my nearly empty water glass, taking a swig.

"You two are gross," Allie says, pushing the chair out from the table. She grabs her plate, taking it to the sink to clean before heading for the living room.

I'm relieved when it's finally just the two of us.

From the table, I get a decent view of Allie. She grabs her virtual reality headset and straps it on, securing it. At least now she can't see us and probably can't hear us, either, with the volume turned up.

"You should really keep an eye on her when she's playing online with other people," I say.

"I still can't believe that you're Bearded Bad Boy," Sadie says with a genuine laugh.

"How'd you figure it out?"

"The star tattoo," she says, gesturing at my chest. "It's the same one on your profile picture."

I reach for my glass of water, wishing it was something a bit stronger. I finish the last few sips. I don't tell her how the tattoo symbolizes being a member of the bratva. If she hasn't discovered that secret, then I don't want to be the one to tell her.

"You should bring your headset over sometime. We could play together," she says.

I don't answer her comment. It's not that doing something together wouldn't be nice. The reality is that I only have the headset to make connections with shady businessmen. The actual time that I've spent gaming is minimal.

"We could, but I have a few other ideas that might be a little more fun."

Sadie chuckles under her breath. "Careful, Allie is in the next room over."

I doubt she can hear anything we're saying with our voices low and the audio on her VR headset turned up.

"I brought dessert," I say, standing to retrieve the chocolate-covered strawberries and cherries. I wasn't sure which she'd prefer, so I opted for both.

My phone buzzes in my pocket, and I grab it and answer the call on the burner phone.

"Hello," I say. There's only one person with the number.

"I've got good news. I tracked them down to a small town in Montana. They are in a remote cabin in Breckenridge."

I exhaled a breath that I hadn't realized I'd been holding.

"That is good news."

Sadie's eyes are on me as she stands to clear the dishes. I shake my head, wanting her to leave the cleanup for me to do.

"Do you have an exact location? An address?"

"I'll text it to you," he says. "And you should know, Nikita is the link. His wife has a sister in Breckenridge."

"Thanks." I end the call and help Sadie with the dinner dishes.

"Everything okay?" she asks, glancing at me from the sink.

"I have a lead on the man who shot me."

"What?" The drinking glass slips through her hand and smashes against the floor, splintering into tiny shards.

Groaning, Sadie bends to pick up the slivers. "Shit." She curses under her breath as a tiny sliver of glass gets embedded in her hand. Sadie hurries across the hallway to the bathroom, slamming the door shut.

Between the slamming bathroom door and Kona barking, Allie removes her headset. "Is everything —" She doesn't finish her sentence.

"Keep the dog out of the kitchen," I say, instructing Allie on what to do. "I'll clean up the glass after I check on your mom."

Allie grabs Kona by the collar and drags her into her bedroom, locking the dog safely out of harm's way.

I give a prominent knock on the bathroom door. "Sadie?"

"Yeah," Sadie says with a groan.

"Let me in. I can help bandage your hand."

There's movement on the other side of the door, and the lock clicks, allowing me to enter the bathroom. "It's open," she says.

Her palm is face up. She's got a set of metal tweezers on the sink and an open bottle of rubbing alcohol beside it.

Kona continues barking from the bedroom, and I close the bathroom door to help silence the noise.

I take her hand that's injured, bringing it closer to my face to examine the injury thoroughly. There's no blood because the tiny sliver is still nestled in her palm. It's small, the size of a splinter, but I'm sure it hurts like hell.

"I tried the tweezers, but I'm not left-handed."

I reach for the tweezers and promptly remove the tiny glass sliver within a matter of seconds before running her palm under running water.

Her cheeks are rosy, and sweat glistens on her forehead. "You're okay," I say, offering her a reassuring smile. I've seen far worse injuries. Hell, so has she, when I was shot.

"Bandages?" I ask.

She points to the medicine cabinet, and I open it and retrieve a small bandage to affix to her hand.

"All better." I bring her palm to my lips and place a kiss on her bandaged injury

"Thanks, Dmitri."

"Of course." I brush a strand of hair behind her ear, my gaze never leaving hers. "I need to clean up the rest of the glass. I think Kona wants out."

"She probably does," Sadie says. "What were you saying about knowing who shot you?"

The woman doesn't miss a thing. I probably shouldn't have said as much as I did, which was next to nothing.

"I don't remember who shot me per se, but I recall who I was in the car with before it happened."

"And you're sure it's someone you know? I mean, it wasn't an accident?"

"That's what I need to find out." I don't tell her there was little chance of it being an accident. The fact that I was sent with Nikita to take out Anton and Savannah makes it an unlikely scenario.

"Did they say where he is?"

She's full of questions this evening. "A small town in Montana." I open the bathroom door and head back toward the kitchen to clean up the shards of glass before anyone else gets hurt.

Sadie is right on my heel. "And you're going to visit him?" There's a hint of fear in her tone. She doesn't know what it's like to be afraid, have your life on the line, or be at the edge of death.

"That's the plan," I say. Bent over in the kitchen, I clean up the broken glass, one shard at a time, careful not to cut myself. After I've gotten every piece I can visibly see, I'm still not confident it's safe. "Do you have a vacuum I can use to make sure I didn't miss any tiny slivers?"

"Of course," Sadie says. She hurries off down the hallway and retrieves the vacuum. I'm grateful it's a bagged vacuum to circumvent any further injuries.

I vacuum the kitchen floor, ensuring it's safe enough for Kona to walk on or lick. After we're both satisfied it's fine, Sadie lets Kona out of the bedroom.

"Where does the vacuum go?" I ask.

There's a smirk on her face as she eyes me up and down. "I'll put it away later. Just leave it in the corner against the wall," she says. "Allie, did you feed Kona?"

The teen groans and then scurries off to feed the puppy before taking her for a walk.

"Are you sure she's all right out there alone?"

I couldn't imagine letting my thirteen-year-old out at night alone if I had a kid. Although it's not an unsafe neighborhood, I can't help but worry about her, especially since Sadie works for the Italians.

"She's fine," Sadie says, and then shifts uncomfortably on her feet. She's second-guessing her decision. "Should I be worried?"

"How about I keep an eye on the two of them?" I suggest. "You can get dessert ready."

I head for the front door and slip on my shoes.

"How do you suppose that I get it ready?" Sadie asks.

"You could bring it into the bedroom." I head out the front door before catching her reply.

ELEVEN

SADIE

I let Dmitri whisk me away on his private jet, although it's far less romantic than it sounds. We stop in Nova Scotia to drop Allie off for the week while we head to Breckenridge to investigate what happened the day Dmitri was shot.

It sounds dangerous, and I'm grateful that Allie is safe with her aunt and cousin while we take a detour to Montana.

A detour that is technically in the opposite direction.

I owe Dmitri big time for having us drop Allie off with family. She's happy to spend time with Olivia, and I'm grateful for some time away from home.

I can't fathom how Dmitri could pay for a private jet, but it was clear that he didn't own it and had to borrow it from his boss. Is that the man who owns the strip club?

Damn, the pay must be nice for a private jet, even if he's only part owner. It's still rather impressive.

"You're awfully quiet," Dmitri says as we come in for a landing.

"I don't like flying," I say. However, the worst is usually my nerves with getting through airport security, worrying about missing my flight, or long delays on the tarmac.

I could get used to flying private, not that I can afford it.

"Even in luxury?" Dmitri asks, raising an eyebrow.

"This is nice." I lean back in the plush leather chair. It swivels and is unlike anything on a commercial plane. "Your boss didn't mind loaning you the plane?"

"One of the perks of the job," he says with a laugh. He must be good friends with his boss.

After we land, Dmitri has a rental car ready and waiting for us. He opens the trunk, tossing our bags inside before coming around to the passenger side to open my door.

I expect the drive to take hours since we're in the middle of nowhere, but that doesn't seem to be the case. In a matter of minutes, we're pulling up at Blue Sky Resort. It's a ski resort, although it's too warm to ski this time of year.

The outside of the building is freshly painted in bright blue and white. Did they remodel the place?

I step out of the vehicle, and Dmitri escorts me inside.

He already has reservations and acquires two room keys, handing me one of them. Not that I plan on exploring the town without him. The only reason I'm in Montana is to make sure that he's all right. After everything the man has been through, making him come here alone doesn't feel right.

He doesn't have anyone.

And for some reason, I want to be his someone.

Which is crazy since we're just friends. Friends who sometimes sleep together and go on fake dates to help each other out. That's what friends do, though, right?

After we check in to the hotel room and drop off our bags, we head out to grab dinner. It's getting late, and I'm starving. "When are we going to that address that you have?" I ask.

"Tomorrow."

I have no idea what he's planning to do when he sees the man who might have shot him. It had to be an accident. Right?

Why leave Dmitri? Did the shooter think that he'd go to prison for murder?

And I swear I heard two gunshots ring out. Had the other shot been fired into the ground?

There was only one body.

My head swims with the different possibilities from that day.

We settle on a restaurant on the mountain, which gives us a nice, scenic drive as the sun sets. My phone buzzes in my purse, and I grab it, glancing at the caller. It's work.

I'm surprised that I get reception out here.

"Hello?"

Antonio's voice is recognizable to me. He's not directly speaking into the phone. Did he accidentally dial me?

"You crossed me. You've given me no choice but to take matters into my own hands," Antonio says. A man is begging for his life, crying and hysterical. A gunshot rings out through the phone.

I shriek and hang up.

"What's wrong?" Dmitri asks.

My hands tremble, and my stomach is spiraling. "Pull over. I'm going to be sick."

We're climbing the mountain, and there's not much space to pull over. But he stops the engine, and I whip open the door, jump out, and vomit on the side of the road.

He puts the engine in park and steps out, coming around to check on me.

I wipe my mouth with the back of my hand.

"Are you okay?" he asks.

I open my mouth, but the words don't come.

My phone rings, and I jump involuntarily. My hands shake as I stare at the caller ID, indicating that it's again Antonio.

This time, Dmitri sees who called. He grabs the phone from my hand and answers the call. "Can I help you?" Dmitri asks.

There's silence for a moment, and then his top lip snarls. "She can't come to the phone," he growls, and his chest puffs out, his back straight and tall. He's ready for a fight.

I watch in horror and hold out my hand, wanting him to hand me back my phone.

"I know who you are, and I don't give a fuck. You don't scare me. Sadie is under my protection. If you come anywhere near her, I'll kill you."

Another beat, and I swear I'm growing nauseous again with dread.

"I work for Mikhail Barinov," Dmitri says.

Is that supposed to mean something to Antonio? I certainly don't know who Mikhail Barinov is. I can't hear Antonio's response, and Dmitri is unreadable.

And what does he mean I'm under his protection?

He ends the call, and I'm unsure if he hung up on Antonio or if the call was done.

"What the hell just happened?" I ask. I fold my shaky arms across my chest. My eyes are wide, unsure I'm comfortable with what Dmitri just did for me. He's trying to help, but I'm not sure he didn't just make things worse.

"There's no fucking way you're going back to work for that asshole."

I don't want to go back to work for Antonio. Not after what I heard. He murdered someone in cold blood.

I wish I were wrong, but by the look on Dmitri's face, he wants to shout from the top of the mountain, *I told you so*.

"He just shot a man," I whisper, trying to catch my breath. My heart continues to pummel against my chest. "Shouldn't we call the police?"

"And tell them what, exactly? You don't know where he is, who got shot, and trust me, you don't want to involve yourself with the Italians further."

He shoves my phone into his pocket and rubs my back in soft, soothing circles. The sun has set, and it's growing darker by the minute. The vehicle's headlights are on, the engine running, allowing us to see the road. "We should get you something to eat."

Seriously? I just threw up whatever I ate for breakfast. I'm no longer hungry. Food is the furthest thing on my mind. "I don't think I can eat."

"Soup. Crackers. Something to help clean the taste out of your mouth."

He does make a good point. I could use it to rinse my mouth. "Yeah."

Dmitri escorts me back to the vehicle and opens the door. He waits until my seatbelt is secure before shutting the car door and coming around.

I stare out the window, watching the trees breeze by on our way up the mountainside. Dmitri stops at a log cabin restaurant in the middle of nowhere. The sign outside reads *Lumberjack Shack*.

Climbing out of the vehicle, my feet are shaky, and my legs wobble, but I know I'm safe. I'm far from New York, and Allie isn't home, either. I don't need to worry about her this week.

All I can think about is the sound of the gunshot. Flashes of the afternoon when Dmitri was shot flicker through my mind too.

I'm frozen, unable to move on my own. Dmitri steps around as he climbs out of the vehicle and accompanies me, his hand around my waist as we step up the wooden stairs.

He doesn't wait for the server to seat us. He finds us an empty booth and helps get me situated before he grabs two menus and sits across from me.

"Thanks," I whisper, the menu on the table in front of me, but I can't focus on the words. It's like a foreign language staring back at me.

A waitress comes to the table, bringing us water and relaying the specials. I excuse myself for the bathroom, wanting to rinse my mouth and clean up.

A few minutes later, I return to the table. Dmitri sips his scotch and gestures toward the alcoholic drink on the table for me. "I took a chance and ordered you an Amaretto Sour."

I gladly reach for the drink, wanting to burn away the memories of the past hour.

"To forgetting—" I wince at my choice of words. I haven't even touched my drink yet, and I'm making an ass out of myself.

Dmitri smiles. If he's offended, he's hiding it well.

"To forgetting the last phone call," he says, and clinks my glass.

I lift the amber liquid, which helps kill the taste in my mouth. I'm grateful for the drink and finish it in a matter of seconds. I gesture the waitress over, but it takes her a minute to make it to our table.

"I ordered dinner for you as well," Dmitri says. "Homemade soup. But if you want to order something else instead, I'm sure we can still change the order. Or add to it."

"Soup sounds good." I'm not sure I can eat much, but spending a few minutes forgetting about Antonio and work will hopefully be enough to help bring back my appetite.

The waitress comes to our table, and I order another Amaretto Sour while Dmitri orders another scotch.

"Tomorrow, you can stay at the hotel when I visit Anton and Savannah. It'll be safer for you if you're not with me."

"Safer because they want you dead?" I ask.

The pulsating music keeps anyone from overhearing our conversation. There's a small crowd, mostly hanging out by the bar.

"I can't be certain they won't try again," Dmitri says. "And besides, you don't need to go through another traumatic event after tonight."

I exhale a shaky breath. "I'll be fine tomorrow. I'm just... I wasn't expecting to hear Antonio take a man's life."

"It can be difficult to witness," Dmitri says.

"Are you speaking from experience?" I can't imagine that he is, but he's been on the opposite end of the barrel of a gun.

He sips his scotch and gives me a wry grin. "How's your stomach?"

Is he intentionally changing the subject or trying to take my mind off the shit-show night that we've had?

"I've been better, but honestly, what you did for me was sweet and reckless."

"How's that?" Dmitri asks.

"You practically told off a mafia boss. I mean, if what you say is true." And I have less reason to doubt him after Antonio's unexpected and unintentional phone call.

"What I say is true?" he repeats.

"You said that I'm under your protection. And you mentioned your boss, Mikhail. What does he have to do with any of it? How do they know each other?"

Any hint of a smile vanishes from his features. His gaze hardens, and he sits straighter in the booth. "Old family. Mikhail's baby sister married Antonio."

"Talk about complicated," I mutter.

"You're done working for Moretti's Bar. If you need a job, you'll come wait tables or handle drink orders at Club Sage."

"That's a strip club."

"Do you have a problem with where I work?" Dmitri pins me with his stare.

"No, just that I'm not going to be taking my clothes off for any man—"

"You're right. You're not going to take your clothes off for any man but me," he says.

I shiver and hope that he doesn't notice. There's something about his dominance that stirs a fire deep within me.

"We're not dating," I say, reminding Dmitri that I don't belong to him. I'm not his girlfriend. We're solely friends.

"We're not, but maybe we ought to be," he says. "Don't stress over it right now. Just know that I will protect you, no matter what."

My lips part and a soft puff of air escapes past. The room is warm, and I reach for my second drink that the waitress brings to the table, swallowing it all back.

I'm confident that I'm flushed, and I don't care. My eyes gaze down at his chest. There's one button that's half undone, and I want to finish removing it and help him undress.

Dinner is brought out, interrupting the moment between us. I'm grateful that Dmitri ordered for me. The bowl of soup looks delicious, and I doubt I could stomach much more tonight.

I'm both tired from the flight and exhausted from the ordeal with Antonio. Quietly, I eat my soup while Dmitri chomps down on a sandwich. Both of us are eating considerably light tonight.

After dinner, we head back to the resort. Heading down the mountain, the resort is lit up, making it easily viewable from a distance. It's like looking at the Vegas Strip from afar, except it's one building in the middle of nowhere.

It's grandiose.

We head inside our room. There's only one bed, which is fine with me. It's not like we hadn't shared a bed before or slept together.

I grab my pajamas from my bag and bring them into the bathroom to change. I brush my teeth, and by the time I'm finished, Dmitri is already in bed, the covers pulled up to his waist. He's not wearing a shirt, and I can't figure out if he's got anything on underneath the blankets.

Dmitri has the bedside lamp on, and I shut off the other lights. Pulling back the covers, I don't admit that I'm disappointed that he's wearing boxers, although they could easily come off. But after the night we've had, I wouldn't blame him if he didn't want to kiss me.

He flips the light off when I'm shuffled under the covers, lying beside him.

"Goodnight," he whispers. The bed shifts as he rolls around and drapes his arm across my waist.

"Night," I say. I lie on my back and turn my neck, glancing at him. The room is pitch black, making it impossible to see his face just inches from mine.

———

I awaken early and roll over only to find the bed beside me empty. The sheets are cool. My eyes flash open, and I realize Dmitri is in the bathroom showering.

Rubbing the sleep from my eyes, I climb out of bed and am relieved when the bathroom door is unlocked.

I slip into the bathroom and strip down.

"Sadie?"

"The one and only," I say with a smirk as I slide the glass door open and climb into the shower stall with him.

He pulls me against him and growls before our lips crash. My fingers tangle in his hair as his hands grip my waist, clinging to me as though his life depends on it.

Maybe it does.

I saved him once.

His cock is hard, poking me, demanding attention.

I drop to my knees, my lips taking him in while my fingers tease over his balls.

"Fuck," he mutters, bracing his hand against the shower stall.

I stare up at him, and a wicked smile crosses my face, loving every moment with him. My tongue drags along his shaft, and he grabs a fistful of my hair with one hand, his fingers tangling in my tresses.

Each breath he takes is more pronounced. Ragged.

"Sadie," he croons. He won't last much longer. And I'm happy to oblige. I take him deeper into my throat, swallowing everything he has to offer.

We finish showering together, his fingers soaping every inch of my body, his touch possessive as he marks and claims me for himself. He bites my neck, nipping at my flesh, fingers curling inside my aching center, bringing me toward the edge. Again. And again.

It's heavenly, and my legs are shaky as we turn off the tepid water. Dmitri wraps me in a fluffy white towel and then grabs one for himself to dry off.

"What's on the agenda for today?" I ask, knowing he wants to confront the man who shot him. I can't see anything good coming from it.

If the man knows that Dmitri is alive, won't he try again to murder him?

My insides are twisted, and my hands tremble as I get dressed. I keep my concerns to myself. Dmitri would have come here alone if I hadn't insisted on tagging along.

He shouldn't be alone.

Hell, I don't want him to be alone. I like him more than I should for a friend with benefits situation.

I like him a lot.

We have the rehearsal dinner and wedding swiftly approaching. I don't want to be his fake date. I want it to be real between us. What we share doesn't feel fake. And he brought it up last night, but I remained silent.

After we get dressed, we have a quick breakfast before Dmitri drives us back up the mountain. He's following the directions on his GPS through the winding and curvy road until we pull up outside a small log cabin.

Dmitri kills the engine.

There's an SUV parked in front of the house. There's no garage or anything frivolous. Woods surround the property on the mountain.

I unbuckle my seatbelt and open the door.

"Wait," Dmitri says. His voice is rough. He clears his throat. "You should stay in the car."

"I didn't come all this way with you to sit in the car." I ignore his request, and he grumbles under his breath as he steps out.

Our feet crunch on the gravel. We're not quiet on our approach, but it doesn't seem to matter. No one comes barreling out with a weapon threatening us.

I'm not quite sure what I expect to happen, but silence isn't it.

Dmitri heads up the wooden porch stairs and gives a prominent knock, waiting for someone to answer.

I'd think they could be at work if there weren't a car in the driveway. It is a weekday.

The lock clicks, and a woman with long blonde hair pulls open the door. Her blue eyes meet mine before landing on Dmitri.

"Dmitri," she whispers, and her eyes flicker. Her hand falls to her baby bump protectively.

"Savannah," Dmitri says, his nose twitching as he glances past her. "Is Anton home?"

She doesn't answer his question, but given that he isn't storming toward the door, I'd guess he's not there.

"How did you find us?" Savannah asks, taking in a sharp breath. She stands her ground at the front entrance, not inviting us inside. Her eyes rake over Dmitri, but it's not intimate. She's examining him, looking at him for something.

A weapon?

"It wasn't that difficult. I hired a private investigator. Nikita's wife has a sister that lives in town," Dmitri says. "Katie."

"Shit," Savannah mutters under her breath. She shakes her head. Her complexion pales. Sweat glistens on her forehead. "Have you come on Mikhail's orders?"

Mikhail.

Why would the club owner want Dmitri to find the two of them? Dmitri was shot.

I take a tentative step backward, trying to piece everything together in my head. Is Mikhail behind

Dmitri's shooting? If that's the case, why does he still trust him? Why the hell does he work for him?

"I came here for myself," Dmitri says. "I want to know who the fuck shot me. Was it you or your pretty little boyfriend?"

Savannah's lips turn upwards in a wry smile. "You don't remember?"

Dmitri's hands tighten into fists at his sides.

If he remembered, we wouldn't be here, trying to help him recover the day that he was shot.

The blonde continues speaking, her eyes tightening on him. "You and Nikita came after Anton. The bratva wanted me dead, and Anton spared my life by risking his."

"The bratva?" I whisper, my voice catching in my throat.

Savannah raises an eyebrow and glances from me to Dmitri. "Don't tell me. You didn't mention that you work for the Russian Bratva?"

I step back, stumbling down the porch steps, but I don't fall.

Dmitri has been so wrapped up in me staying away from Antonio because he runs the mafia that he neglected to mention that he's no better.

I hurry through the forest, running on foot. I don't have keys to the vehicle to leave Dmitri's sorry ass behind.

TWELVE

DMITRI

Fuck! That did not go as planned.

Sadie takes off on foot when she hears that I work for the bratva.

"Thanks a lot!" I shout at Savannah. "Now look what you did," I snarl at her. I gesture toward the forest. "It's not bad enough that your boyfriend shoots me, but you have to ruin the one good thing I have going for me!"

"Anton didn't shoot you," Savannah says. Her voice is calm, her demeanor much more relaxed than she should be, considering her condition.

Not that I'd harm a pregnant woman, but she should be scared. If I found her, the bratva can as well.

"Then who the hell did? You?" I shouldn't be surprised, considering that she's FBI. Well, she was an FBI agent when she met Anton. She was an undercover agent and turned him.

"You don't remember," Savannah says. She's taking her time and glances past me at the forest.

I follow her gaze. Sadie is out of sight.

The bitch was buying time to keep Sadie from me!

I don't give a rat's ass anymore who shot me. Sadie is gone. In the forest, and who the hell knows where she is? There are grizzlies in the woods, and she's alone.

I turn on my heel and hurry in the direction Sadie went as I chase after her.

"Nikita shot you!" Savannah shouts at me as I rush away from the cabin.

I don't want to comprehend what Savannah said because I was betrayed by one of my best friends and closest allies. However, I trusted Anton as much as Nikita. My stomach flips, but it's not from the news of who tried to kill me.

There's no sign of Sadie.

"Sadie!" I shout, searching the forest, looking for any signs of where she went and what direction she traveled.

There are multiple broken branches, but they head in two separate directions. There's another cabin to the west, visible over a small bridge and stream of water.

Could she have run to the neighbors for help?

I don't want to involve anyone else if she didn't go pounding on their front door.

Fuck.

There's no sign of her, only the sound of the water trickling through the forest. The riverbed is considerably dry. There's no chance Sadie was swept away or decided to walk through the water to avoid her footprints being seen.

I spin around. The cabin where Savannah lives is still visible. Sadie had to have traveled farther into the forest. I keep walking, unsure if I'm heading in the right direction. She could have climbed a tree or found an enclave to hide inside.

I retrieve my cell phone from my pocket. I surprisingly have a decent signal. I've got one shot. If she turns off her phone, I won't be able to find her.

I pull up her name in my contact list and hit call. In the distance, I can hear her phone. The sound bounces off the trees and landscape. I hurry in the direction before the ringing ceases, and when I try again, it goes directly to voicemail.

I don't leave a message.

What would I say?

I'm not about to admit that I work for the bratva over the phone. That's a conversation to be had in person.

Vehicles are passing through the forest. There must be a road up ahead.

Not twenty minutes later, I step out of the clearing. There's no visible sign of Sadie. Had she hitchhiked? Did she stay in the forest? Maybe she's walking down the mountain?

I can't keep looking for her. She could be anywhere, and it's obvious that she doesn't want to be found.

I walk down the mountain road and recognize the entrance to the cabin where Savannah and Anton live.

Savannah's vehicle is still parked in front of the house.

I yank my keys from my pocket and jump into the front seat. I head down the mountain, keeping an eye out on the road for any sign of Sadie.

She's nowhere in sight.

I make my way back to the hotel, not expecting to find her in the room, but I'm hopeful.

She isn't in the hotel room. Her clothes remain untouched. Her belongings were abandoned like she had last left them. I stop by the front desk and find out where I can purchase some necessities for hiking and camping.

I'll need a flashlight if I end up in the forest when the sun goes down. If I encounter a bear, I'll need bear spray.

There's a shop at the resort, and I stock up on essentials along with a few snacks and bottles of water. I drive back up the mountain to the cabin and knock on Savannah's door again.

"I haven't seen her," Savannah says. "Did you try calling her cell phone?"

I exhale a heavy sigh. It's already been a few hours. I'm worried that she's lost and won't know her way out.

"Yes, she turned it off," I say.

"Or she blocked you. What's her number?"

I give Savannah her phone number, and she dials, waiting. Her eyes light up when she answers.

"Hello?"

Savannah puts her on speakerphone but holds up a finger to warn my ass to remain silent. We don't want to spook her.

"Sadie, where are you?" I can't stop myself.

Savannah glares at me to shut up.

"I don't know," she says. Leaves are crunching, and a growling sound is in the background. Her voice tremors. "I just found two baby cubs near a cave."

"Get out of there," I warn her. "The mother will be protective of her young."

"I—" The phone goes dead.

Sadie could be anywhere.

THIRTEEN

SADIE

Running into the middle of nowhere wasn't the brightest decision I've ever made. Worse, coming face-to-face with two bear cubs when looking for shelter.

Their mama isn't far behind.

She growls as I retreat, keeping my head down. I don't know much about bears, but with dogs, you don't want to challenge them. I assume it's the same when it comes to a menacing stare.

I avert my gaze and walk backward with long strides, doing my best to escape the mama bear before she attacks.

My cell phone fell from my hands and smashed into a tree limb lying on the ground. It's useless. I don't know where I am or how I will get out of the forest.

Being lost is my second concern. The first is the aggressive bear stalking me.

With every step I take backward, she takes two steps closer.

I have nothing to throw at her. Nothing to make loud noises to scare her away. I'm no longer near her cubs, but she doesn't seem to care about that, only that I was near her babies.

I don't want to be a threat, but it's too late.

Begging and pleading aren't going to save me.

I take another step and trip over a log, landing on my ass.

The mama bear takes the opportunity to lunge at me.

I grab a rock from the ground, throwing it at her.

It's not enough.

I scream, find another rock, and throw it at the bear.

In the distance, the sound of a gun goes off.

The bear is fixated on me.

I scramble against the ground, scooting backward. I can't jump up to my feet without coming face-to-face with the grizzly.

The bear is agitated. Angry.

She swipes at me as I scurry backward, and she jumps onto me. I'm confident that I'm done. It's over. I'll never see Allie again. My sister will have to raise her. They say your life flashes before your eyes.

Two dark orbs of the bear's eyes and sharp teeth stare down at me. The bear grabs my hair, yanking my head while I scream in horror.

This is it—the end.

Another gunshot.

My eyes close, the pain from my head and the bear's weight crushing my chest.

———

I awaken to the sound of beeps—soft cotton sheets. And a stiff mattress at my back. My fingers run over the fabric as my eyes flutter open.

"She's awake," the blonde says, gesturing for Dmitri to come back into the hospital room. He's carrying a steaming cup of coffee. His eyes are filled with worry.

Savannah isn't the only one at my side. I don't recognize the man, but he has his hand on her shoulder. Is that Anton?

"Good to see you awake," the stranger says. "I'll let the doctor know."

"Thanks, Anton." Dmitri puts his cup of coffee on the side table and comes toward my bed, his hand finding mine. "You gave us quite a scare."

I nod and wince from the pain. It could be worse. My insides feel crushed, and my head throbs, but I'm alive.

"How bad is it?" I ask. I haven't seen my reflection. Do I have scars from the bear attack?

"You've been out a couple of hours, but the doctors aren't concerned. A few bruised ribs and a mild concussion."

"That's it?" My hands shake as I rest them on my lap.

"You were lucky that Savannah knew where you were. We took the four-wheeler to track you down and stop the bear from attacking you."

"Did you kill it?" I ask. I can't help but worry that the cubs won't survive without their mama.

Savannah pats my arm. "You're lucky to be alive. A few more seconds, and we wouldn't be visiting you in the hospital."

I exhale a sharp breath. I'm angry with him for lying to me and hiding his identity, but I can't stay mad at him forever. He did save my life.

The doctor comes into the room and quickly examines me, ensuring I feel well. They want to keep me another day for observation.

The doctor leaves, and Savannah pulls Anton to follow. "We'll give you two a minute."

I'm not sure that I want to be alone with Dmitri. I'm torn between anger and love. It's a strange feeling.

Dmitri sits in a nearby chair, pulling it closer to the bed. He reaches for my hand, but I pull away as quickly as he tries to touch me.

"I'm sorry I didn't tell you who I worked for, but I didn't want to involve you in anything dangerous."

I huff under my breath. "That's absurd," I say. "I found you shot in the forest. I'm involved, Dmitri."

His tongue darts out and swipes his top lip. "You are," he admits, and expresses himself with a heavy sigh. "I want to keep you and Allie safe. From the mafia to wild animals in the forest. I can't do that if you won't let me near you."

He glances down at my hands, and I allow him to touch me this time. It's a simple gesture, not overly intimate.

Baby steps.

"I don't plan on going into any more forests, ever again. I'm a city girl." I want to fly back tonight. I miss my home and my bed. I never thought I'd feel safer in New York City than in a small town, probably because New York doesn't have grizzlies.

I'm not sure I'll be able to sleep without nightmares.

"I love you, *Malishka*. All this pretending to be a couple has made me realize that you're the only woman I want in my life."

"I'm a package deal. Allie and me."

"Even better," he says with a growing smile. "Does that mean you'll take me back?"

It's not that simple. He lied to me. Kept secrets. Why does he think I'll eagerly jump back into his embrace? Sure, the sex was dynamite, and I enjoyed being around him, but that was before I discovered he worked for the bratva.

What else hasn't he told me?

"I d-don't—know," I stammer. "You hurt me. Lying to me, you broke my trust."

I half-expect him to defend himself. To tell me that it wasn't a lie, it was an omission. "You're right, Sadie. I'm sorry. I'll do better. I won't keep secrets from you."

FOURTEEN

DMITRI

Montana was a fucking nightmare. Between Sadie being attacked by a bear, discovering I work for the Russian Bratva, and learning from Anton that Nikita was the man who shot me, my world has been turned upside down.

Sadie is doing considerably well. Her injuries aren't visible. She seems to have overcome the concussion, and the bruising on her ribs will take time to heal. The doctor instructed her to do no heavy lifting, take it easy, and rest.

I carry her suitcase to the private plane as we head back to pick up Allie and return to our lives in the city. I'm looking forward to going home, except I don't know what that means for us.

She hasn't boxed me out like I thought she might, and we still have much to talk about on the flight home.

Us.

The bratva.

Her job working for the Italians.

She can't go back to the bar. It's too dangerous. Now that Antonio knows she's *mine*, he could use her to get to us. It wouldn't be the first time they've caused us trouble.

She sits across from me, and a quietness fills the air as we take off. I wait until we're at cruising altitude before unfastening my seatbelt.

"We need to talk about what's going to happen when we get home."

Her brow furrows, and she presses her hand to her head like she has a headache. "Do you need something for the pain?" I ask. The doctors had given her a few prescriptions should she need them.

"No," she says, and leans back, trying her best to relax in the white leather chair. "Go on," she says, gesturing for me to continue.

"I meant what I said the other day about protecting you."

Her brow is furrowed. She doesn't seem to remember or thinks I'm referring to the bear attack in the forest. It's been a long couple of days.

"Antonio isn't going to like the association between us, friends or otherwise," I say. While I want to make her my girlfriend and keep her entirely to myself, I respect that she's been through a lot and may not be ready to commit to anything.

"Yeah, I recall that I lost my job. Again." She pins me with a look, and I shift uncomfortably under her scrutiny.

"I told you, Nikita will hire you as a bartender or waitress."

"You can't know that," Sadie says. "You haven't even spoken with him."

She's right. I haven't chatted with him or called him while in Breckenridge. It wasn't safe for Anton and Savannah.

Nikita betrayed Mikhail and his brothers.

Anton and I had a tense discussion while Sadie was in the hospital. He assured me he just wanted to be left alone, given a second chance with Savannah.

And Nikita, as wrong as he might have been in shooting me, had done it to protect the family.

Mikhail had fucked up and acted without merit, demanding Savannah be executed when he had bedded and brought home an FBI agent himself.

While I may not have agreed with Anton, I appreciated his candor and perspective on the situation.

And given that they helped Sadie, I no longer held a grudge against them. Besides, they weren't the ones responsible for shooting me.

Nikita, on the other hand, I have words for him when I see him at the compound or the club.

"Nikita will hire you," I say, my gaze never leaving hers. "He's responsible for shooting me, and if he doesn't want Mikhail to find out that he meddled where he didn't belong, he'll do what I ask."

"You're going to blackmail him?"

"That's one way of looking at it," I say. That wasn't my intention, but I understood he was giving his friend a second chance.

I was lucky that I got my second chance, that Sadie found me, or I'd likely be dead.

Sadie is quiet and contemplative. "What about Antonio? Do I need to worry about my daughter? Should we be considering leaving New York for someplace else? I don't want to live somewhere woodsy where there are grizzlies, but Chicago or Los Angeles would be safe."

I reach for her hands, intertwining our fingers together. "You don't need to leave the city. I told you that I'd protect you."

"You can't be around every minute, Dmitri. I need to know that the mafia isn't hunting down my daughter."

"Marry me."

"What?"

I smile and laugh at the horrified look on her face. "Relax."

"Now you're going to suggest we have a fake marriage?" She shakes her head. "You're too much."

"That wasn't what I was going to suggest." I do want to marry her. One day. It's too soon to jump in, but I want her to know that my family will protect her. And I need the Italians to see that she belongs to us.

"Well?" She waits for me to elaborate.

"You and Allie move in with me. I live at the compound with other members of the bratva."

"Dmitri, no."

"Just hear me out," I say, taking her hands and giving them a gentle squeeze. "They are my family, and they will protect you. They'll die for you. And more importantly, Antonio won't come anywhere near the house."

She exhales a heavy breath. "You two are enemies?"

"That's right. And between you overhearing the hit and him discovering we're together, you will be a target. I can continue to keep a security detail watching your apartment, but I can't promise that he won't come and harass you. I'm sure he knows where you live since you work for him."

"Oh, he definitely knows where I live. He met my daughter," Sadie says with a grimace. "I stupidly let him inside my home to use the bathroom."

"You did what?" My hands clench into fists as I stand and pace the length of the small plane. "He met Allie?"

"Briefly," Sadie says. "I didn't think anything of it."

"He could have put a surveillance bug in your apartment. I'll have one of our men sweep the building as soon as we're back. Unless you're willing to join me and live under my roof."

She purses her lips, considering the request. "It's just a bunch of grown men? That doesn't sound healthy for Allie."

"There are other families living in the compound. Some of them have children. Allie will be the oldest of the kids, but I'm sure she'd fit in. She'll have her own bedroom, and we'd share a room."

"And your boss would be okay with that?"

"He would if we were engaged," I say.

Sadie opens her mouth, and I swear she's about to protest.

"We don't have to set a wedding date," I say. "But our engagement should be enough for me to convince Mikhail to bring you and Allie home with me."

"Can I think about it?"

"Of course. But I want you to know," I say, bending down in front of her seat and taking her hands in mine. It's not a proposal. I don't have a ring, and I doubt she'd say yes. "I'm doing this because I love you and want to spend my life with you and your daughter."

FIFTEEN

SADIE

If Dmitri had proposed, I'm not sure I would have said yes. But I care about him more than I should for a fake relationship.

And the funny thing is, nothing about us feels fake. It never has.

After we pick up Allie from Nova Scotia, I give her the news without telling her everything. She doesn't need to know that the man I've fallen in for is with the Russian Bratva.

That's a secret I don't think my thirteen-year-old daughter can keep.

She's ecstatic to hear that we're back together and that we'll be living in a new house. Although she has a lot more questions than I have answers, I've promised her that we'll take it one step at a time.

"This house is so big!" Allie says. Her mouth drops as we head past the wrought iron gates and guard entrance.

"Our family lives here. All of us, under one roof," Dmitri says.

"Like your parents and grandparents?" Allie asks.

"My brothers."

"That's so cool! I wish I had siblings. It would be neat to live with them when we grow up."

I exhale a nervous breath, not wanting Allie to probe any further regarding Dmitri and his family. She's an intelligent young girl and bright enough to figure out that these men aren't biologically related to him.

"Are you sure that it's okay for us to stay here with you?" I ask. I don't want to be a hindrance.

"I insist. And I've already contacted your neighbor who is watching Kona. She'll be dropping him off this evening." Dmitri pulls up out front of the main entrance and puts the vehicle into park. I step out. The mansion is clearly on two lots and is well maintained.

Dmitri opens the trunk and retrieves our luggage from the trip. We've already discussed having to return to the apartment to pack up our belongings, but he's insisted that he will have movers handle everything. We're not to return to the apartment unless he's accompanying us.

Allie admires the outside of the building, standing out front, staring at the intricate trim, décor, and architecture. "Wow."

"I know. They say the outside has real gold trim," Dmitri whispers a little too loudly to Allie.

Her eyes light up. "Really?"

Dmitri shrugs. "That's what I've heard."

I smile, watching the two of them interact. He's good with Allie. She's never had a male figure in her life and to think the men she'll grow up around from this point forward will be members of the bratva is frightening.

But if they're anything like Dmitri, then it won't be so bad. I like him a lot, which explains why it was so easy for me to agree to move in with him. I have my doubts, but he's promised to protect me, and with the Italian Mafia lurking in the shadows, this is the safest option.

Allie slides her arm into his, letting him escort her inside. He leaves the luggage by the front entrance and gives us a tour of the interior.

The house is magnificent. The staircase on the right spirals up to the second floor. Dmitri gives us a tour first of the downstairs, introducing us to the other children and their mothers in the playroom, before showing us the dining room, kitchen, and bathroom.

The tour continues upstairs. Dmitri grabs our bags. He doesn't let me carry anything, and he's right. I need to let my ribs heal after the bear incident.

Dmitri shows Allie her bedroom, and next door is our room. Relief floods through me that her sleeping arrangements are close by.

She plops down on the mattress, glancing around the barren room. There's a dresser opposite the bed and a nightstand, but not much else.

"Can I decorate it?" she asks.

"If you want to put posters on the walls, I'm sure that's fine."

"What about paint?" A wide grin spreads across her face. "I've always wanted to paint my room, but I couldn't because it was an apartment."

Dmitri offers a warm smile. "That will be our first order of business."

"Really?" Allie's eyes light up.

"Tomorrow morning, we'll drive to the store, and you can pick whatever color you want for your bedroom."

"Awesome!"

"Thank you," I whisper, reaching for Dmitri's hand, intertwining our fingers together. I appreciate everything he's done, including his boss hiring me to work at Club Sage as a bartender.

———

After dinner, Allie seems to be settling in, reading a book in her new bedroom with Kona curled up on her puppy bed.

Dmitri has offered to buy Allie a bookshelf that she can fill with as many books as will fit if she promises to read them. The girl is in absolute heaven.

"Walk with me," Dmitri says, and takes my hand, leading me downstairs and through the back door. There's a lush garden in full bloom with lights illuminating the path and wrapped around the roof and legs of the pergola.

It's pretty beautiful.

The sunset was quite some time ago, but it's difficult to see the stars with all the light pollution from the city.

"How are you doing?" Dmitri asks. He leads me to a wooden bench, and we sit.

"Sore, but otherwise, I'm okay. Are you sure that we're safe from the mafia?"

"I promise you that Antonio and his men won't touch you. You have nothing to worry about, *Malishka*."

"Thank you." I breathe a sigh of relief. Antonio is still out there, but with the protection of Dmitri and his brothers, I trust that my daughter and I will be safe.

"I was worried about you in the hospital." His fingers push back a strand of hair, tucking it behind my ear.

"I'm just glad you could find me before it was any worse." I cringe at the memories that flood through me. I shouldn't have run recklessly into the forest. I could have been lost for days, starved to death, or he could have been two minutes longer, and I'd have been mauled to death.

Dmitri's hand is on my back in soft, soothing motions, and I rest my head on his shoulder. "Almost losing you made me realize that I don't want to live without you in my life."

I rest my hand on his thigh. "I almost lost you before I even knew who you were," I whisper, thinking back to the day I found him shot on the forest floor.

"I love you," Dmitri whispers.

I tilt my head toward him, shifting slightly as I brush his lips against mine, taking it easy and slow. His kisses are always passionate, and I can't be wild and unabandoned with need and desire while I'm healing.

"I hate... taking things slow."

Dmitri chuckles, tears filling his eyes with laughter.

"What?" I ask, not understanding why he's laughing so damn hard.

"I thought you were about to say I hate you."

I frown, confused. "Why would I say that?" That's the furthest thought from my mind and untrue.

I'm not happy he lied to me about who he works for, but I would never have let him anywhere near my daughter or myself. And I'd be working for the Moretti family, and having discovered Antonio's secret, my daughter and I would probably be dead.

"I don't know," Dmitri says with a laugh.

"Well, it's not easy for me to say, but I do heart you."

"You heart me?" he asks, raising an inquisitive eyebrow. "Is that like the next step before love but after like?"

"It might be," I say with a smile, and chew on my bottom lip. "I've never been in love, not the type you're referring to. Obviously I love my daughter, but that's different."

"Understandably so."

"What about the man who gave you Allie?" Dmitri asks.

"He's hardly a man. The minute he found out I was pregnant, he left."

Dmitri snarls. "Coward."

"I've learned over the years not to rely on anyone. It's probably one of the reasons that I hadn't dated anyone until you."

"Thirteen years? Does that mean you've been celibate for that long?"

I press my lips together, and the air feels warm outside. Am I blushing? At least the darkness hides the color in my cheeks. I glance down at my lap, avoiding his heated stare.

"You don't have to answer that," Dmitri says. "It's none of my business."

I'm relieved, and while I'd likely tell him anything that he wants to know, it's also embarrassing. "You're the only man I've ever had a fake relationship with and a real orgasm."

His jaw drops, and he laughs. "I don't even—are you telling me that you normally have fake orgasms with your real relationships?"

I smile and give a faint nod.

"That's no good," he growls, and leans closer, his lips crushing mine.

I whimper, not from pain but from need.

He pulls back. "Did I hurt you?"

"Gosh, no," I whisper against his lips. My insides are pulsating with need. He has the uncanny ability to make me weak at the knees. "But we have to take it slow."

He lifts me into his arms, carrying me toward the house.

"Dmitri, put me down!" I squeal with laughter, grimacing from the pain of my giggles.

He obliges. "I'm only putting your feet down, so you don't hurt yourself further." His insistence is cute, and I want to kiss him until the sun comes up and our bodies are intertwined together as one.

Perhaps going slow isn't the worst thing in the world. We can truly savor every moment as we grow together into a family.

And I think I might be falling madly in love with him.

Maybe I'm just too scared to admit it aloud?

EPILOGUE

DMITRI

Weeks ago, I pulled Nikita aside after visiting Anton in Breckenridge.

Nikita came clean about everything. He felt awful and guilty having shot me and thought for weeks that I was dead. It had given him nightmares that only Lucy had known about.

I understood what he did, wanting to buy time for Anton and Savannah to escape. He didn't mean to betray the family, just as Anton hadn't meant to with Savannah.

And while it hurt that he hadn't trusted me and chose them, all of it led me to meet Sadie.

The universe had a crazy plan for my happiness, and I would accept it even if I were still bitter about being shot and left for dead.

Mikhail was kept in the dark about Anton and Savannah's whereabouts. Nikita and I agreed that it would be safer for all parties involved. And Mikhail had been out of line, deciding that he acted too hastily without enough information.

I hadn't fully understood the situation at the time. I'd been given orders by Mikhail and followed them.

No one would dare tell the pakhan he fucked up. He was in charge, and the weight of what he had done would weigh on his shoulders and those of his men, believing that he had done what was necessary to protect the family.

Nikita had done what he thought was necessary as well.

"Are you ready?" I ask, knocking on the bathroom door, giving Sadie her privacy while she gets dressed for Luka's wedding.

The bathroom door finally opens, and Sadie steps out in a deep purple dress. It's knee-length with a skirt that flares out. Her hair is curled and pinned at the sides. She is gorgeous, and she's all mine.

"Should we see if Allie is ready?" Sadie asks.

"The kid's been done for twenty minutes."

"I'm not a kid!" Allie quips from our bedroom. She's seated at the edge of the mattress, waiting as patiently as a thirteen-year-old girl can, considering that she's antsy as hell to go downstairs for cake.

She's asked four times when the happy couple will cut the cake and she can have a slice.

"You're right. I'm sorry," I say to Allie, apologizing for calling her a kid. She is Sadie's kid, but she's not a child. "I should have said the young lady has been done for twenty minutes."

Allie beams proudly and steps down from the mattress, testing her new black heels. They're not too tall and platforms, but she's still unsteady.

I offer her my arm, and she gladly takes it. "Thanks, Da—Dmitri," she says.

I glance at her, curious about the slip-up. Was she about to call me dad? My chest swells, but I don't want to push. It's only been a few weeks with Sadie and Allie living with me.

One step at a time.

Sadie steps out of the bathroom and leans against the wall while she slips on her heels. "I'm ready."

I gesture for Sadie to walk out of the bedroom first as I help Allie navigate the stairs. I don't trust that the girl won't fall since it's her first time in heels.

Allie leans into my ear once her mom is several steps ahead of us. "Weddings are super romantic," she whispers. "Are you going to pop the question tonight?"

I smile, grateful the kid, or rather the young lady, has my back and wants me to become a permanent part of their family. "I don't want to take away from Luka and Hannah's special day," I say.

Allie nods thoughtfully. "Good point. When you do, you have my permission."

"Thanks, kid."

"It's young lady," she snaps back with a wry grin.

———

Thank you for reading Dangerous Boss. I hope you loved Sadie and Dmitri's story.

Do you love bossy billionaires? What about grumpy single dads? The hot new contemporary romance series features Clare and Levi in BILLIONAIRE GRUMP.

I am Levi Luxenberg. 40-year-old billionaire. CEO of Luxenberg Enterprises. And apparently, father of one.

A week ago, having kids wasn't even in my 10-year plan.

Now, I have a 5-year-old daughter who will hardly look in my direction.

I am aware that Amelia is grieving her mother's death, and I swear I'm not a complete jerk, but I jumped on a private jet to Chicago at a moment's notice, and the kid won't even say a word to me.

As if that wasn't bad enough, our pilot just got sick and I have to fly commercial for the first time in years.

You'd think that would be the end of it, but, no.

The cherry on top?

Amelia would rather interact with Clare, the divorced, jobless, tipsy woman sitting right in front of us, than me.

She chats with her, she smiles at her—she even draws her a freaking picture.

I would be really mad if I didn't actually need a nanny. Urgently.

Since my assistant screwed my ad over and made me look like a grumpy billionaire desperately looking for a wife, Clare suddenly seems perfect for the job.

She has no place to live, no idea who I am, and no qualms about being my live-in nanny on a trial basis.

The problem is, I think I might want to keep her around longer...

One-Click BILLIONAIRE GRUMP today!

Sign up for Willow Fox's newsletter

And I'm thrilled to offer a sneak peek of SECRET VOW, a spicy dark mafia romance with a happily ever after.

The way she dances does things to me that I know are wrong.

I swallow back another glass of whiskey, trying to suppress the urge to stalk over and capture her lips with mine.

"Tell me you're not considering sleeping with Nicole DeLuca," Moreno says.

He's my second, my best friend, and also blatantly honest, even when I don't want him to be.

He also knows that I've sported a hard-on for Nicole since the moment I learned of Gino's daughter.

I like a challenge, and she's off-limits. It makes the catch that much more fun.

"Have you seen me so much as talk to her?" I shoot Moreno a glare to shut the hell up. Somehow, I doubt he will do as I want.

He's a good guy if such a thing can be said about the Ricci Family.

"You keep drinking and staring. She's bound to notice you," Moreno says.

Maybe that's the point. I want her to notice me. I want her to fear me like her father, Gino, fears my family.

Nicole struts onto the dance floor. The light cascades across her raven hair.

She bumps and grinds, arms tossed into the air.

I want to fuck that smile right off her gleeful face.

She's a force to be reckoned with, and I'm just the man to turn her life upside down.

"Have another drink. It's on me." Moreno gestures to the bartender, and he waltzes over and pours another whiskey.

"On you?" I laugh.

I own the damned bar.

He can offer to buy me all the drinks he wants. I drink here for free.

"Doesn't mean you shouldn't tip the staff." Moreno slides a fifty to the bartender, Ren-something.

I forget her name. I hired her after the last guy caused me a headache and a dead boss.

Some things are better left in the past.

Being don has its advantages, including getting any girl I want.

Tonight, that girl is Nicole DeLuca.

I shift on the barstool.

Usually, I claim the corner booth. It has a reserved placard for the occasion that I might want to come in and have a drink or business with an associate.

"You need another girl. Someone less deadly," Moreno says.

I laugh under my breath and sip my whiskey. "You talk like she's an assassin."

"Her father is."

I wave my hand in the air. "He's an old man, Gino. Pain in my ass." He is also a problem that needs taking care of, but that's a job for another day.

Tonight, I'm here to cut off some steam and have fun.

"You fuck that girl, and he'll hunt you down," Moreno warns. He gestures the bartender over and gets himself a drink.

I raise an eyebrow. I haven't seen Moreno drink in, well, since forever.

This is bad if he's drinking. "Shit, I'm driving you to drink. It really must be the end of the world," I mock.

He pinches the bridge of his crooked nose. He got that from defending my honor in a bar fight nearly two decades ago. I'd been young, naïve, and on the cusp of seventeen. I knew how to fight like a kid, not like a man.

Moreno rectified that. He taught me everything I know about the family business.

"Just promise me that you'll leave her alone." Moreno sips his whiskey.

It's obvious to anyone who knows him he can't stand the taste, but he drinks like a pro to an outsider.

"You don't have to kill yourself for me," I joke and point at the whiskey. "I'll down that if you're struggling."

"Do you see me struggling?" Moreno asks.

"While you enjoy that whiskey, I'm going to work my moves on the dance floor."

"Dante," Moreno says my name, but his tone holds more than just a hint of warning.

He's screaming at me to listen to him.

But when do I ever listen?

The funny thing is that I'm his boss, and I don't take orders from Moreno or anyone else. While I appreciate his concern, that's all it is to me, and I'm going to do whatever the hell I want.

Hasn't he realized that yet?

I climb off the barstool and make my way onto the dance floor. I don't dance. There's no need.

I'm on a mission, and she is my target.

We lock eyes, and she blushes on my approach.

Good. She doesn't seem to know me. At least she hasn't indicated that I'm the bastard trying to kill her father.

"I'm here with friends," she says like that line will work to shoo me away.

"Nice of them to ditch you," I say.

She's been dancing for the last forty or so minutes, alone. The handful of guys who tried to pick her up haven't had any luck.

One of them looks at me apologetically.

I've yet to see her with a shot or drink in her hand, either.

"How do you know they're not in the bathroom?" Nicole asks.

"If they are, they must have snuck out the window."

She rolls her eyes. "Are you implying that I'm that boring?"

"On the contrary, I'm implying nothing, only that you're a pretty woman dancing alone."

"I'll bet that line works on all the other girls," Nicole says.

She's right. It doesn't take much for them to fall at my feet. I'm blessed with good looks and a great body. Does she not notice?

"How about I buy you a drink, and if you never want to see me again—"

"Okay."

Her response takes me by surprise.

I lead her toward the reserved booth and gesture for her to climb in first. The booth is curved, and I make sure to sit close beside her, our thighs touching.

I want to touch her, seduce her, and bring her all sorts of heightened pleasure.

"Are you sure we should be sitting here?" Nicole asks. "It did say reserved."

I merely shrug. I don't want to give away who I am, especially if she's unaware of my position of power. She shouldn't know.

"Let's see what happens," I say.

She raises a curious eyebrow but shuts her mouth.

The bartender from earlier comes over, and I gesture for two drinks—one for each of us. I don't have to give the bartender my order. She gets the finest liquor, top-shelf from the collection.

"I never got your name," Nicole says.

"Daniel," I answer. It's a lie. I've always been Dante.

It's clear she doesn't recognize me, and I can't have my name triggering any further recognition.

"I'm Nikki," she says and rests a hand on my thigh.

Her tune has changed since I met her minutes ago on the dance floor, but I'm not sure why. Do I care?

"It's lovely to meet you, Nikki," I say, as if I'm trying to remember her name.

I could never forget it. I've had my eye on her since she strolled into town and moved in with her daddy, my number one enemy: Gino DeLuca.

All I've wanted is to take him down, and in the process, I'll be forced to ruin her for other men.

Too bad.

She's beautiful, with her long black hair and deep-set amber eyes.

Cute and sexy.

And she could have a normal life if I wasn't at war with her old man.

The lights are dim, the bar not terribly crowded for a Friday night.

The music slows, and I'm glad we're already in the booth. While a slow dance is nice at times, it doesn't fit right now. Not when I want to grind against her.

The bartender returns with two drinks. One is a whiskey for me and the second a whiskey sour on the rocks for her. It's strong but sweet, too girly for my taste, but the ladies haven't turned it away in the past.

I don't expect her to be any different.

But I'm wrong.

She slides her glass toward me and grabs mine before I can lift it to my lips. "I'll have what you're having."

She means my glass of whiskey.

Damn, that shit is expensive.

The girls always get the off-label, and since it's mixed, they can't taste the difference.

She smiles coyly and bats her long, dark lashes, but it's just an act.

What game is she playing tonight?

"Hope you don't mind. I prefer the good stuff, liquid gold." Nicole gulps the whiskey in a matter of seconds and slams the glass down hard on the wooden table.

Her warm amber gaze has flecks of gold, and the longer she watches me, the more I fall into her stare.

What the hell is going on?

"Do you want to get out of here?"

I do more than anything, but my gut is telling me no. "How about I take you back to your place?" I suggest.

I already know she's living with her father, but I wonder what excuse she'll give me.

One Click SECRET VOW now!

ABOUT THE AUTHOR

Willow Fox has loved writing since she was in high school (many ages ago). Her small town romances are reflective of living in a small town in rural America.

Whether she's writing romance or sitting outside by the bonfire reading a good book, Willow loves the magic of the written word.

She dreams of being swept off her feet and hopes to do that to her readers!

Visit her website at:

https://authorwillowfox.com

Dangerous Boss

Bossy Single Dad Series

Billionaire Grump

Mountain Grump

Bachelor Grump

Ice Dragons Hockey Romance

Faking it with the Billionaire

Daring the Hockey Player

Looking for kinkier books? Try these spicy stories written under the name Allison West.

Boxsets

Academy of Littles

Western Daddies Collection

Obey Daddy Collection

The Alpha Collection

Western Daddies

Her Billionaire Daddy

Her Cowboy Daddy

Her Outlaw Daddy

Her Forbidden Daddy

Standalone Romances

The Victorian Shift

Jailed Little Jade

Prefer a sweeter romance with action and adventure?
Check out these titles under the name Ruth Silver.

Aberrant Series

Love Forbidden

Secrets Forbidden

Magic Forbidden

Escape Forbidden

Refuge Forbidden

Boxsets

Gem Apocalypse

Nightblood

Royal Reaper

Royal Deception

Standalones

Stolen Art